THE REAPER COMPLETE SERIES

Books One to Five

BLAK RAYNE

ALSO BY BLAK RAYNE

The Ideal Side of Love

The Ideal Side of Life

Carson's Story

Older the Better

The Jock

Tease to Please (multiple authors)

Turkish Delight

Put Your Ho Ho's On (multiple authors)

Reaper Series

Kiss the Reaper

Maximum Kill

Jack the Anthropophagite

Apprentice Killers

Embrace the Reaper

The Reaper Complete Series

Coming to eXtasy Books

Radioactive

DEDICATION

In fond memory of friend and author Michael J., I miss your unprecedented
support, passion for the written word, and sound advice.
And to everyone who has read my stories, thank you.

WELCOME TO Z'S WORLD

Whenever I wrote from Brody's perspective, he seemed to take control. So even though Z is the main protagonist, maybe I should say, 'Welcome to Z and Brody's World' instead. Speaking about perspective, if you're new to this series, you will notice the viewpoints switch from chapter to chapter. Sometimes it's Z, who is always first person POV, and sometimes it's Brody, third person limited. Alternating between the POVs wasn't done to confuse, but it had everything to do with how my muse wanted their story written. And, now that it's come to an end with this anthology, I'm almost sad to let go of these two wonderfully complex men.

KISS THE REAPER

Book One

CHAPTER ONE

*E*very Friday night he'd visit the seedy hotel on Barnes Street, room 216. He was tall, wiry, and clean-shaven—an artificially serene gaze behind a pair of silver-rimmed glasses—and attractive, in a geeky sort-of-way, with his raven hair parted on the left and a long bang covering his right lens. Initially, his baby face and youthful charm seemed harmless. But closer inspection revealed much more behind the glasses, an indestructible force of nature swirling in the depths of his steely-gray eyes. A person's appearance can mask the truth, and when we'd first met, I was certain his masked a multitude of sins.

In the beginning, I performed as trained. I got down on my knees and attempted to give him a blow job, but he stopped me. The second time he came to my suite I tried everything to entice him, even offered to masturbate. But the thirtyish man who wore a neatly pressed suit, gray dress shirt and leather tie never wanted sex.

He'd sit beside me brandishing a razor-sharp smile and talk. I couldn't complain. He was a paying customer. Fifty an hour or five hundred for the night and, as per routine, he paid cash. The entire twelve hours sealed in an envelope black as his suit, which he placed on the nightstand under the lamp.

Gradually, I became accustomed to Brody's odd behavior and didn't bother to solicit any services other than a customary greeting. We'd chat as if we were in a posh restaurant, whiling the hours away over an extravagant meal. Then, at the break of dawn, he'd leave. He seemed like a nice enough man, perhaps someone trustworthy. Which was the very reason I tried not to tell him much about my past. I didn't want to jeopardize the relationship we were building. Our get-togethers had become the highlight of my existence.

The ugliness had begun in my childhood. Desperate for a hit, my drug-addict mother sold me into the sex trade at the ripe age of twelve, and shortly after she died of an overdose. At the time, her pimp Gino took me in. He'd said he had a soft spot for kids, and since I needed to eat, I'd have to earn my keep like every other whore.

There were only two good things about Gino—he always paid, and he never hit me. As long as I serviced the clientele, he left me alone. But then I wasn't the typical prostitute; all his workers were women, where I was a scrawny effeminate-looking man. The fact I *was* a man didn't seem to bother Brody. He still came to see me once a week, he still talked, and he still paid. And Friday nights were his.

"It rained hard today." He locked the door. "Made my job difficult."

"Yeah, and ah...what is it you do?" I put the ashtray on my chest and blew smoke rings. They rose toward the ceiling, stretching until they were gone.

"I'm not permitted to say."

"Aww," I whined, "but that's boring. We've known each other for a while now, and you've never told me anything about yourself."

"That's for your safety as well as mine." He stood near the grimy window, removing his blazer, and for the first time, I saw his guns. They were semi-automatic pistols, and bigger than I'd imagined. He slid the holsters over his shoulders and hung them on the only chair in the room along with the jacket. Loosening his tie, he motioned to the bed. "May I?"

"Sure." I shifted to give him space and he flopped out next to me, arm behind his head. The man never did casual, so my curiosity was piqued. "Tired?" I asked.

"A little. But I also want to be near you."

"You sure you don't want a massage or something...? You look tense."

"I'm good." He switched to lie on his side and bunched a pillow under his neck. "I like being with you."

"Me, too." I mashed out the cigarette. "Are you one of those plainclothes detectives?"

"I work for the pharmaceutical corporation, End Life."

Everyone knew about End Life. Their medical ads were splashed on huge billboards throughout the city. What I couldn't figure out was why a drug company would hire a man who carried guns. Obviously, whatever Brody's line of work, it couldn't have been one hundred percent legal.

He touched my cheek. The backs of his fingers were cool and smoother than I thought they'd be. Then he leaned toward me. Stunned, I held onto the ashtray as he kissed my lips. It was the first real, affectionate gesture he'd ever made. After that, he drifted to sleep. No explanation, nothing.

I put the ashtray down and carefully removed his glasses. His expression remained peaceful. I held the frames to my eyes. It was odd, but the lenses didn't distort my vision. I wondered why a man would wear fake glasses. Then I had to remind myself Brody was a john, and that meant his personal life was none of my business. It went against the rules to pry. Any type of real, intimate contact could cause a serious problem since neither of us were free men. But that didn't stop me from wishing for more—man or not, I wanted to spend all my time with him.

I set the glasses on the nightstand, shut off the light, and got comfortable.

Sometime during the night, I woke to the pale, orangey-hue of a streetlamp and a kink in my neck. The other side of the bed lay empty, the pillow plump and sheets neat, as if no one had slept there. I frowned.

As usual, he'd departed without any warning. Angry, I kicked the covers aside, stood naked in front of a tarnished mirror glued to the wall and combed my mop. I despised my frail build. No muscle. Unattractive. Puffing out my chest, I tried to enlarge my pecs, but quickly exhaled the wisp of a miserable sigh. Got dressed, shoved the money from the envelope in my jacket pocket, and put on my sneakers.

The shadows in my suite obscured everything, except for a bright thread of light outlining the door. Scarcely blocked by the paper-thin wall, pellucid voices resonated from the next room. Curious, I pressed my ear and palms to the wall. The voices were male—Gino's raspy timbre and Brody's soft rumble. Brody should've gone long ago.

"Who owns the prostitutes?"

"I do," Gino replied curtly though he sounded nervous. However, Brody's tone didn't waver.

"Then who employs you to run this hotel?"

"I don't know who you are, buddy—"

"Answer the question."

I heard a sliding and click and Gino stammered, "Okay, okay! Look, the hookers are mine, all right, and I lease this dump from the Calabrese gang. I pay two grand a month for the building and thirty-five percent of all my profits in exchange for the protection they offer."

I wasn't the brightest bulb in the pack, but even I knew to dish out that kind of money every thirty days had to be nerve-racking. It wasn't as if the gangs in the East End were known for their charity, especially the Italian criminal organization. They'd done away with more people than the state executioner. Basically, the gangs ran the entire eastern section of the city and kept law enforcement at a controllable reach. Police did patrol in heavily-armed squads of six, but they only dealt with serious crimes—murder and drug trafficking. Other offenses, such as theft and assault, were secondary and didn't warrant the manpower. So, everyone who lived in the area had to rely on the gangs. Mob justice at its finest.

"What about Z?"

Soon as Brody said my name, I clung to the wall, listening more intently.

"He's no different than any other whore in the joint."

"In other words, he's your property as well."

Gino immediately grew defensive. "If it weren't for me, that mongrel would've been out on the street beggin' for change!" I could picture him, sweat beading his bald scalp, a cigar stuck between his yellow teeth, and pointing at Brody. "His mother was a strung out slut—useless at making any decent coin! I told her over and over, 'use a fucking condom!' But do you think she'd listen? Then she gets knocked up! After she died, I raised his punk ass, so yeah, I own him! *Capisce?*"

Right then, the conversation hit a brick wall. Seconds of tense silence passed. Not another word. Not a sound. And I wondered what was happening, or if Brody would shoot the asshole. Easing away, I stared at the chipped paint, waiting. Suddenly, with a muted thud, someone left the room.

CHAPTER THREE

The elevator slid shut at the far end of the hallway and I caught a glimpse of Brody inside. I raced past it and down three levels of a concrete stairwell to catch him. Once on the street, he walked like he had a purpose, cutting straight through anyone in his path. I followed him for several blocks, where he entered an abandoned warehouse in an industrial park. I kept close to the walls and shadows, careful not to disturb anything.

On the fifth floor, in what had once been a spacious office, sat the basics in furniture—a liquor cabinet and kitchenette, bathroom, and a bed—it wasn't how I expected him to live. A meticulous man, he seemed the type who would rent a West End condo.

Brody began to remove his clothes, and I ducked behind a rusted filing cabinet. He wasn't huge or burly, but lean, an unbreakable man, and I felt an even stronger attraction to him. In certain respects, we were one and the same—a pair of freakish oddballs—mutually needy. I wanted his attention and it seemed he wanted my approval. But what about love? And what about sex?

His cock was long and lean like him, his nakedness beautiful. My stomach fluttered and I bottled my breath, quickly looking away to stay calm. He deserved privacy and my respect. But my thoughts were far from respectful.

Water ran, and I waited, rubbing nervously at my sweaty upper lip. The bathroom door opened, and Brody emerged in a cloud of steam, waist wrapped in a towel. In minutes, he was dressed and adjusting his tie in front of the large window. Then he slid the holsters over his shoulders, buckled the chest strap, and put on his blazer.

Once again, he was on the move, myself in pursuit. But somehow within a block of the warehouse, his trail had gone cold.

"Shit," I gasped, my breath misting in the air. Light from a neon sign nearby glistened on the damp pavement. No other business in the immediate area was open. I had a hunch and pulled on the blackened entrance door.

Loud music hit like a brick, rattling my chest. People drank, danced and made out—the club was a den of wickedness. And I soon became disoriented in the chaos, temporarily absorbed like water into a sponge by the hypnotic pulse of lights. I shoved against the suffocating mass of bodies and scanned the sea of bobbing heads. At the rear of the club, I noticed a hallway emitting a red glow and, for some inexplicable reason, I felt drawn to it and moved in that direction.

When I reached it, a man brushed past, bumping my arm. The unnatural light obscured his head and shoulders. I paused and glanced back, but he'd vanished. Our interaction was so brief, only his stature had registered. There were three doors to my left and the middle one stood partly open. I gave it a cautious push and it crept inwards. The red glow from the corridor gradually spread across the floor.

I gagged.

In the center of the room was a dead man, seated on a chair in front of a boarded window, his mouth gaping, a quarter-sized hole in his forehead. He stared with vacant eyes, those deprived of a soul. Blood trickled past the bridge of his nose and had spattered the plywood in the window, like someone had flicked paint from his or her fingertips.

For the first few seconds, I was too traumatized to be scared, but had enough sense to get out of there. Murder was still illegal. Turning on my heels, I blew from the room, heart hammering. I tried to act normal, but failed, wading at an urgent pace across the dance floor, propelling people out of my way. A yard ahead was the silhouette of a tall figure, a man engulfed in the epileptic beat of strobe lights. I don't know why, but the back of his head and shoulders, and his sturdy purposeful gait seemed all too familiar. He had to be the man who'd passed me minutes before.

He exited the building and I did the same, dashing outside into the drizzly night. Gulping at the cold air, I looked in every direction. The street was desolate, not a human in sight—the man had, yet again, vanished into thin air. I turned east for home, an alley sandwiched between the club and neighboring building, and someone materialized from the shadows.

"W-Who are you?" I demanded, limbs shaking.

"Why did you follow me?"

Surprised at the sound of Brody's calm voice, I faltered, and he started to walk toward me. "I overheard your fight with Gino...I wanted to talk to you. That's all, I swear."

Suddenly we were face-to-face, captured within the glow of a streetlamp. Frightened, I backed straight into the nightclub, trying to ignore his advances.

He wore black leather gloves. He removed them one at a time and tossed both in a nearby dumpster. "You were there," he said without intonation.

It wasn't a question, rather a statement, so, I couldn't possibly lie. My vision blurred, and I sniffed, taking an unsteady wipe at my upper lip and nose. "Yes."

"Were you disgusted...? Fearful...?"

The questions were strange and made me nervous, but I answered honestly, "Yeah, at first...but then I thought maybe the guy deserved it."

Slapping a hand against the brick wall, Brody searched my eyes and I noticed his were hauntingly affectionate. "You are *so* enticing." His words resonated to my core. Then he pressed the tip of his index finger to my forehead. "Never let me in because you'll never get me out."

"I think...it's too late." I cast my gaze to the ground.

He traced the ridge of my eye socket and up to the soft spot of my temple. My pulse rose, thudding against his touch. I wanted to scream, and cry, and beg him for sex all at once, but by some means I managed to swallow it all, a tangle of anxiety and desire.

He cracked that razor-sharp smile and continued, following the curve of my cheekbone, as though taking an x-ray, examining me from the inside out, straight through to my flesh. It was impossible for me to move and my breathing came in soft ragged gasps. I slowly but surely slipped into his world, a dark and lonely place ruled by terrifyingly unstable logic, or so I thought.

Then, he kissed my cheek and blew my fear right out of the water. The fondness was the last thing I'd anticipated, not that I knew what to expect, and all of a sudden, I came to the realization I was in love. Somehow, I'd fallen for a monster. And that monster was the only being in the whole world who had accepted me—a hooker, damaged goods.

It definitely is too late.

"Is something wrong?" he asked.

"I don't want to do it anymore, Brody."

"Then don't." He dug inside his blazer and handed me an unopened pack of butts. "I meant to give them to you earlier."

"Thanks." I accepted the gift wholeheartedly since my nerves were shot. "I still can't believe...you seriously killed that guy." Rain hit my face hard, like minuscule bullets. The weather had switched from cold to wet and freezing. I didn't know why, but whatever apprehension I'd felt before, dissolved, and I could face him.

His mouth curled into a childish grin as if he was extremely pleased with himself. "It's what I do. Does it bother you?"

I shrugged and lit a cigarette. "Each to his own...I guess."

"Let's get out of the rain."

~

BACK AT MY HOTEL SUITE, I hung my damp clothes over the register and pulled on an old hoodie. Brody lay in a prone position on my bed with a hand on his chest and ankles crossed. With his other hand in the air, he rolled a crimson-and-black marble between his index finger and thumb.

"Are you warm now?" he asked.

"Yeah, I feel much better." I got comfortable next to him. There was a different side to Brody, the flip side. When he looked at me with his half-lidded, steely-gray eyes, I saw an entirely different man, a tarnished, however caring soul, absent of malice. "Where did you get that?"

"End Life." He continued to stare at it. "This is the very first one they gave me."

I snuggled a pillow and watched him intently. "Is it important? Something to do with your job?"

"Yes, to answer both questions. It's called a 'marker.' Inside this marble is the name of my target." He angled the glass and holographic letters imprinted on a ribbon of red glistened. "Simon was my first kill for the corporation. Whenever my services are required, End Life sends an agent to deliver a marker."

The idea of a corporation paying a man to discriminately murder people was like something out of a science fiction novel. He had a scary occupation.

"People like that could turn on you. Aren't you worried?"

"I've never really considered it. But even if they did, I'm well equipped." Resting his hand on his chest, he turned to me with a smile. "I've always wanted to ask...Z is a strange name. Where did it come from?"

I reached inside the nightstand drawer and dropped a paperback on the bed, worn at the edges, its front cover creased. He picked up the book and studied it with care. "Z is short for Zeus.

My mother was big in to mythology. She used to read from that book when I was little. When I grew up, it seemed dumb for a scrawny weakling like me to be called Zeus, the most powerful of the Greek gods. So I told everyone to call me Z."

"He was also the dispenser of good and evil. You should read more, and this book would be an excellent start."

"Why? Do I sound dumb when I talk?"

"It's 'stupid.' Dumb means mute and, no, you don't. You come across as uneducated. However, if you read, that will change."

"I do read...a bit... But I guess not enough."

"The label on a soup tin doesn't count." He grinned.

"That's reading too, ya know. Labels have big words." I quickly seized the book from his hands and opened it to the first page. "I never went to school."

"It's fine. Life is a better teacher."

We talked for hours, and by dawn he'd left. As for me, I festered in the depressing solitude of my suite for days. One bastard after another filtered in and out. But, all I gave were blow jobs—anything else seemed dirty, as if I were cheating on Brody. I couldn't get him or what he'd done off my mind, the sickly-sweet scent of death that had lingered on his clothes, and his calculating nature.

I had a serious problem. Brody and his disturbingly macabre occupation, whatever it was, turned me on.

CHAPTER FOUR

Slouched against the sill, I blew smoke out the open window, watching the rain. Large droplets slithered down the glass. Near the street, a storm drain erupted like a volcano, spilling a muddy deluge. I was waiting impatiently for my best client, as I always did, smoking my brains out and counting the minutes. Finally, someone knocked on the door; I couldn't contain my happiness.

"It's unlocked." I quickly took a last drag and flicked the cigarette outside.

Brody appeared, clean-shaven, and my suite immediately smelled of food. He held out a bag. "I thought you might enjoy a decent meal."

"You didn't have to."

"I know I didn't. But you're far too thin."

"Well, thanks. ...What is it?" I peered inside the bag.

"Italian—spaghetti and meatballs with garlic toast."

"It sounds yummy." I sat on the bed with a bounce, crossed my legs, and foraged inside the white plastic. I found disposable cutlery, napkins, and a packet of wet-wipes atop an aluminum foil container; he'd thought of everything.

He shut the window, positioned the chair in front of the bed, and hung his blazer over it. Then he sat, bent forward, with his forearms on his knees and hands clasped. "How have you been?"

"Okay, I guess. Why?" I twisted the noodles onto the fork then put them in my mouth.

"Has anything out of the ordinary happened recently?"

I swallowed and replied, "Not that I know of. Is something wrong?"

"Word is on the streets the Calabrese gang is restless. Incidents of violence have increased. Their enforcers are hurting people without just cause. Has anyone threatened you?"

I tore a piece of garlic toast and gave him half. "No...well, I mean yeah it happens with some of the johns once in a while...if they're drunk or cranked on drugs before they come see me. But that's normal."

He straightened his posture. "I see. Who picks your clients?"

"No one really. Some are gay and some are curious...most just show up. Either they heard about me from another hooker or a john."

"So they aren't screened?"

"Hell no!" I laughed derisively, swirling the fork again. "This isn't a daycare. And it's not like Gino gives a shit what happens to me. It's hard enough to get the assholes to wear a condom let alone screen them."

I stopped ranting and an awkward silence filled the gap between us.

Brody studied my expression, while eating the toast. Internally, I crumpled. I felt like a totally idiot for lashing out; it wasn't his fault I hated to screw strange men for a living. I hung my head and finished the last meatball then I couldn't stomach another bite.

"I like you the way you are," he said.

"Yeah, 'cause I'm stupid...and gullible."

"On the contrary, you're intelligent and kindhearted, and you're the only person who can tolerate me." He bent closer, lifted my hair away from my face, and kissed my forehead.

Surprised by the affection, I scrunched the bag and said sincerely, "I'm sorry."

"Don't ever apologize for how you feel. I will always listen."

By two in the morning, Brody had passed out on the blankets with one arm slung across his eyes and the other on his chest. I don't know how he could sleep wearing the holstered guns. But he did. I'd curled into a ball beside him, and lightly touched his side. No reaction. His breathing remained heavy. My eyes burned, I wanted to him to love me.

During Brody's next visit, we strolled the streets wrapped in conversation about life. And when the sun broke on the horizon, we watched it rise from a set of six-tiered bleachers in a derelict baseball park. He remained faithful, visiting every week. And I never tired of his friendship, and he seemed just as enrapt with me. He'd become my reason for living.

"What...? You're too good for the rest of us now, you can't spread your legs?" Gino lit a cigar, blew the match out, and dropped it in an ashtray on the table.

"Who said that?" I was surprised anyone had complained. The females did ten times the business in a night—I didn't even come close in sales. Women generally didn't pay for sex, and men who were in to men were few.

"One of the johns complained."

Gino's disgusting girlfriend gawked at me. She was strewn across the bed like dirty laundry with her mini skirt hiked up and bare twat exposed. Her hair a rat's nest and mascara smudged under her eyes, she stunk of cheap perfume and booze, and the sour stench seeping from her pores had filled the room. The lousy old slag was enough to make anyone vomit.

"I don't want to spread my legs anymore," I protested.

He walloped me. Shocked, I held my cheek—it seriously hurt.

"Whatever. You need to earn your keep and you haven't been doing much of that lately. There's a hotel two blocks west of here, the Black Knight. It's in behind that transgender bar. The guy is in room twenty-three."

"I'm meeting the guy somewhere else?" I thought it was odd, but I couldn't go against Gino's orders.

"Don't worry, the guy's a straight shooter. And you'd better not skip out." He pointed at me. "Or your ass is grass—*capisce?*"

"Yeah. I got it." I wandered into the hallway then turned around, reluctant to go.

"Good." He stuck the fat stogie between his teeth and slammed the door in my face.

I'd acted calm, but at my core, I was a bundle of nerves, anxious and apprehensive to leave the safety of the hotel. Something didn't feel right. Gino had never sent anyone to a different location. The clients always came to the Regent. That was the golden rule. But when it came to me, I guess the rules didn't apply.

The Black Knight had no viable qualities. The place was a dump, worse than the shit hole I called home, and infamous for drug overdoses. High above my head, half a wooden sign creaked in the damp breeze, and the glass in the entrance door was held together by thick tape. I stepped inside the lobby and broken fragments crunched under my sneakers and the stench of urine curled my nose. Pinching it, I gagged, and a rat scuttled over debris near my feet. I almost threw up. The only thing on my mind was Brody, and how much I missed him. It was Friday night, the usual time we spent together. Once he realized I wasn't in my suite, I wondered if he'd come for me. In the four months, we'd known each other he'd never let me down, and I'd hoped that night would be the same. I needed his company. It was all that kept me going, the light at end of the tunnel, and my comfort.

The elevator was out of service, and by the looks of it, hadn't run in years. Steel bars welded to the side plates blocked the doors. The only other way to reach the fourth floor was the stairs. I squeezed through the fire exit. Placing my hand on the bottom rail, I peered into the gloom above.

This job is simple. That's what I mumbled under my breath. I had to hear a voice, a voice of encouragement, even if just my own. I'd entertain the guy for a couple hours then I'd leave.

This job is simple.
I slid my grasp higher and climbed the first flight of concrete.
This job is simple.

CHAPTER SIX

The rear exit grated, the brown door streaked with corrosion, and I stumbled into the rain and darkness, an alley littered with filth. My entire body ached, and I could scarcely move. I gingerly pressed my sore hand to the outer wall of the hotel. Feeling the damp brick and rough ridges of mortar, I used them as a guide and shuffled in the direction of the street. Someone bumped me in passing. Knocked off balance, I fell into the adjacent building then slid down the wall and collapsed in a heap on the wet ground. Blinded by tears, I sputtered and cried. Rain assaulted the pavement in waves, the sheer volume deafening, a solid mass of perpetual noise that blocked all other sounds of the city and my sobbing.

When I opened my one good eye, Brody was squatting in front of me, forearms on his knees and an umbrella resting in the L of his neck and shoulder. His expensive black suit was soaked and his highly polished leather shoes beaded with rain. He held out a white handkerchief.

"For me?" I asked, disinclined to accept.

"For you."

I carefully dabbed the corner of my eye, the was fabric soft and smelled fresh. "Thanks... How did you find me?"

"I went to your room and you weren't there. You never go anywhere on a Friday night. I figured something happened."

"Yeah, somethin' happened." My lower lip and chin quivered and I shielded my face with an arm, ashamed to look at him.

"You'll catch pneumonia if you stay here."

"I don't care!"

"But I do." He hoisted me to my feet.

I STOOD in the office bathroom, hair dripping and flesh clammy, as Brody rolled his sleeves and turned on the tub faucets. Water rushed and steam saturated the air. He unbuttoned my shirt, undid my belt, and removed my clothes then helped me into the tub. I didn't speak, but sat, shoulders hunched and arms limp, as he washed my hair. He didn't question me about what had happened —he was smart enough to figure it out, especially when he'd found me lying disheveled in the street. Instead, he talked about his life as if trying to take my mind off things. After a lengthy soak, I dried my hair, and then lay on his bed. He plugged in the space heater.

Getting up on my elbows, I asked, "Do you want to have sex?"

He gently pinned me to the musty old mattress, hovering on all fours. His black hair was scented of the outdoors and rain, and tickled my face. "We can't. You're injured and you're not ready yet."

"What're you talkin' about? You helped me. At least I can repay you."

"You're not a whore anymore. This isn't about repaying me." His gaze filled with displeasure, and then he hung his head, exhaling a heavy-sounding sigh. "From this moment forward, everything changes. I want you to start a new life."

"What do you mean?" I waited, but he didn't answer, and it

hurt. It hurt so bad my chest felt tight. Maybe I'd got too greedy, allowed too many of my emotions to surface. Maybe he didn't like emotional people. He killed people—that's what he did. And a guy who destroyed life wouldn't want to love it. Inside I was falling apart, bitterly confused, and angry. Clenching a fist, I pressed it deep into the blanket and grimaced, fighting back the tears.

He kissed my forehead, climbed off the bed, grabbed his blazer, and was gone. I didn't understand, and a burning ridge of moisture rose in my eyes. I flopped an arm over my face and hollered, "Thanks for fucking breaking my heart!"

CHAPTER SEVEN

Shortly after my temper tantrum subsided, Brody returned with hamburgers and fries. We talked and ate, and then I stayed at the warehouse for over a week—he wanted me to heal. And by the following Tuesday evening, he said I had to go home, but not before I identified my attackers. I wasn't about to question his motive and led him directly to room twenty-three at the Black Knight.

The events unfolded as if in slow motion. Brody moved in precise increments, frame by frame, like the lapsing sections of an old film. He pushed on the door. It swung open. He drew both guns and advanced into a smoky haze fractured by amber light. The men inside the room hollered. A cavalcade of frenzied noise. Earsplitting gunshots.

Bang! Bang! Bang!

I covered my ears, turned away and sank against the outer wall. There were more deafening blasts—a hail of gunfire then abrupt silence. Dropping my hands, I edged cautiously toward the room, fingers gliding along the dirty wallpaper. I couldn't seem to resist the temptation to look like a motorist when they slow down near the scene of an accident. I had to witness the aftermath; I had to experience what he'd done.

Blood smeared the floor, spattering the walls and frost bitten windowpane. A table was overturned, chairs toppled and glass shattered. Playing cards and poker chips were everywhere. And among the mess lay four dead men, the same four men who had savagely beaten, raped and robbed me of my last few dollars and dignity. I turned around and around, staring at it all, trying to comprehend.

Too much blood. Too much death.

Suddenly panic-stricken, I dropped to a crouch and doubled over, holding my stomach. The hoarse, pathetic whimper didn't sound like my own. I strained to yell. Then Brody appeared, a stain against the dull light, pistol at his side, face expressionless.

"You didn't have to do this." I gagged, covering my mouth.

"I just took something repulsive and made it beautiful." He stroked my head as if I were his pet dog, obedient to the end.

I nodded to let him know I understood.

He holstered one gun, tightened a silencer to the muzzle of the other and said matter-of-factly, "What they did to you was depraved. People like that don't deserve to breathe."

Next, we were at the Regent, standing outside its decaying façade under the rectangular neon sign. We used the lobby entrance and took the elevator to the third floor where it stopped dead like a condemned man dropped from the hangman's noose. Brody exited and I warily followed at a safe distance.

Outside Gino's room, he paused and put a finger to his lips. "Wait here," he whispered.

He knocked and when the door opened, he forced his way inside, shoving my fat pimp to the floor like an overturned bowl of jelly. Gino's girlfriend shrieked, Brody shot her, and she slumped over the pillows, blood rapidly soaking through the beige fabric.

Then he stood in the middle of the room, his boots and pant legs glistening red. Gun aimed at my pimp, he looked over his shoulder at me. Gino cowered at the foot of the bed, shielding his head. I didn't want any part of the game. I wanted to run far away, but fate had brought me to this place—fate and desperation for acceptance.

"W-What are you doing?" I asked.

"Setting the record straight," Brody answered coldly.

"You don't have to. ...The other guys," I gestured in the general direction of the Black Knight, "Were enough."

He switched his attention back to Gino, who was a quivering and sniveling mess. "While you stayed at my place, I asked around, and a dozen people told me the same story. Gino sent you to that hotel on purpose so his friends could rape and rob you. They were gangsters he owed money to. You were abused in lieu of his debt. He's an even bigger piece of shit than his dead friends."

Honestly, I knew Gino had set me up—I just didn't want to hear it.

"Trust me, this prick," Brody glared at him, "Isn't worthy of your loyalty."

Gino's sweaty, ashen features caught my peripheral vision even though I tried to ignore him. "Please," he begged, hands in a steeple as if he was about to pray, "Don't let him kill me. You know I wouldn't hurt you, don't you, Zeus? I always took care of you and your mum...took care of you both real well. We go way back to when you were a kid. Didn't I let your mum keep you?"

The humanity in me wanted to spare his life, but the darkness in me wanted to settle the score, and the darkness rapidly won. He was a pathetic little man. Useless. Cruel. And I no longer pitied him.

"Wait! Don't leave!" he cried.

The terror rang clear in his shaky voice, but I didn't look back. If I took one more step, my unspoken command would be obeyed and I'd be freed from the past, free to start a new life. Brody would do anything for me. It felt incredibly liberating to have that kind of power—to exert a little vengeance on someone who had hurt me.

I paused in the doorway. "My mother beat me and you never stopped her. Some of the johns abused me and you never stopped them." I didn't need to see the results and stepped into the hallway. And even though I'd anticipated it, the gunshot still startled me, but somehow, I kept moving.

The adrenaline coursing through my veins drove me to the stairwell and a blinding dash. My footfalls echoed, slapped the concrete. At the bottom, I burst through the exit to the outside and sucked the cold in, in great gulps, freezing my lungs. The winter air was crisp, and my limbs trembled violently.

Moments later, the same hinges creaked and I sensed Brody's presence. For a split second I wanted to run, my mind reeling—Gino was dead. But then Brody touched my shoulder and I latched onto him. I didn't care that the smell of death mixed with his cologne and gave him a sickly-sweet odor. I only cared about him and what he'd done for me.

He wrapped me in a warm embrace. "Now you're free," he said. "Free to do whatever you choose."

CHAPTER EIGHT

"*N*ow you understand. I'm not like you, Zeus."

"Who are you? Really? I need to know the truth."

We were at the warehouse with the small space heater running. It did nothing but warm a ten-foot radius while the rest of the room remained chilly. I sat on the edge of the mattress to the sag of worn springs.

"I executed my first kill at sixteen." He settled in the chair across from me and it faintly creaked. "She was a high school class-mate who bullied the other students for personal enjoyment. One day her bullying went too far and another girl was severely hurt. The incident ruined her life. After that, I sought out the evil, the people who corrupt."

He claimed he didn't kill for self-gratification but out of a sense of duty. Twisted as it sounded, he saw himself as an avenging angel, righter of wrongs, some kind of divine vigilante. Whatever he was or perceived himself to be, there were things I'd witnessed for certain—when he killed, he always remained calm and focused with no physical sign of emotion. He was fearless in the face of uncertain odds.

"How many?"

"Hundreds."

"So you're like a...serial killer then." I wasn't surprised when he didn't deny it.

"Everyone calls me 'the Reaper.'"

"Why the Reaper?"

"I harvest souls."

"You'd never come after me, right?"

"Never." Brody's indomitable gaze connected with mine, and for some bizarre and unfathomable reason, I felt a sense of lasting peace. "You're the only person who makes me happy. Anyone else I could rip to shreds."

The words were cold as ice, a frightening narrative from the man I'd grown to love. But I accepted his confession.

He rose from the chair and began to undress. "I'm going to have a shower."

"Sure."

While he was preoccupied, I could've run away. But it seemed a cowardly thing to do after everything he'd done for me. I didn't know much about love other than no one, not even my mother, had ever cared about me like Brody did, unconditionally. It didn't matter that I was a whore—he'd protected me.

I always slept in the nude and draped my clothes on the chair. Digging through a crate of musty magazines, I picked one that seemed interesting and got comfortable in the mountain of pillows.

He wandered from the bathroom, drying his hair and stopped dead, his expression that of mild shock.

"Is something wrong?" I flipped a page, trying not to stare at his crotch.

"I was positive you would've left."

"Nope. I'm reading."

"I *killed* Gino, Zeus." He'd emphasized the word *kill* as if I had no concept.

"I know that."

For the first time, I saw a sparkle in his eyes, an inkling of desire when he asked, "How's the reading coming?"

"Yeah, it's okay...best as I can manage. There are big words I had to sound out."

"That's normal. The more you read the better your brain will get at deciphering the difficult words."

"What does tour duh force mean?" I looked up from the magazine. "'Cause it says here," I poked the page, "The man in this article is some dictator who was a tour duh force."

"It's pronounced *tour de force* and it means the dictator accomplished something that required great skill."

"I don't think it means that. It says he was a *tour de force* on the battlefield and wiped out the opposing army."

"To put it in simple terms he triumphed over his enemy."

"Oh." I grinned, and then affirmed, "He was a force to be reckoned with...someone kinda like you."

The faintest smile fractured Brody's cool features, an indication he was quite pleased, but his eyes never changed, they were lifeless as always. He hung his towel over my clothes and slid the chair closer to the space heater. "There are two others like me." He cozied in next to me, flipping the covers and the bed sunk lower. "Serial killers nurtured and exploited by End Life."

"I don't understand." My dick was rock hard and I wanted him to touch it—to touch me everywhere. *Why is he naked?*

"End Life isn't just a pharmaceutical company, Zeus. They have several divisions and one has substantial government backing."

"Is that the division you're from?" I set the magazine in my lap, concentrating on his every word. I had to do something or I'd pounce on him.

"Yes. I was part of a project called Snuff. In the last thirty years the number of violent crimes has steadily increased, and with prisons overflowing, the courts have nowhere to send the criminals. Snuff was meant to lower the number of criminals— exterminate the unwanted in society. How it works is the agents are told a location to leave the markers. I don't see them and they never see me. It is a straightforward system...at least it was until recently. Now the names I get are for criminals leaving the prison, those who have paid their debt to society, the homeless, and others."

"And you're worried because it's wrong."

"Not worried, but disturbed. The normal pattern has changed. I have never killed anyone innocent before."

"Why are you telling me all this?"

"If they discover we're together, your life will be in danger." He bent an arm behind his head. "So I want to give you ample opportunity to leave. I won't stop you. End Life can't have their top killer feeling empathy. Emotions pose a risk. I may second-guess my next order or worse, spare the target." He shifted onto his side and rested his head on my chest, hugging me. "I have killed for you, Zeus. You've changed my perspective."

Everything he'd said made me happy and I couldn't ignore my feelings. "I told you I'm staying."

For the first time, a serial killer had found a way to care beyond a demented, self-gratifying view and I was the object of his desire. If Brody had genuine feelings for another human being, he'd no longer serve a purpose, but pose a viable threat. End Life couldn't have him thinking and questioning its agenda, he was a loose cannon.

His raven hair was soft between my fingers and he appeared different without his glasses—angelic. My beautiful angel.

"I want to make love to you." He kissed my chest then shifted his weight, inching a bit lower, shoving the blankets out of the way. My hairs stood on end, triggered by the moist trial of his saliva cooling on my belly. "I'll take it slow," he said, nuzzling the base of my stiff cock.

I'd slept with countless men and they'd seen me naked. But when Brody looked at me I felt self-conscious, and pushed at his head, begging, "Don't touch it, it's dirty."

"It isn't dirty, it's beautiful." He gently moved my hands out of the way.

My cheeks were on fire and I was dying of embarrassment, but I surrendered nonetheless, wilting against the pillow.

He pressed a finger, cold with lube, against my opening. Pinching my ass, I expelled a groan, the anticipation tingling from my anus straight to my cock. I watched as he sucked me off—his mouth didn't do half as much as his finger did, plunging deep inside me. Then, staring at me, he added a second and finally a third, his fingers fluttering my prostate until I couldn't handle anymore. And just as I was on the verge of ecstasy, he removed his fingers, ran his warm lips up my thigh, kissed my knee, and got into position. Wrapped me in his arms, arms that were sinewy and strong, and murmured against my cheek that he wanted to hear my voice.

And then I cried into the darkness like a woman, dazed by my emotions and his pulsating heat deep inside me. He'd taken something from me that no john ever had—he'd consumed me body and soul, right down to my fingers and toes. Chin tilted, I closed my eyes, concentrating on the feeling. The bed bounced and the old, rusty springs squeaked.

He kissed my Adam's apple.

"Ah...yeah, right there." I raised my hips to his. "More..."

He grunted, pumping faster, and our damp skin slapped. The headiness of his excitement scented the air. And his meaty girth rubbed the right spot. I moaned and my passage tightened. I tried to hold everything in, but all the desire I'd kept hidden burst from my heart, blinding me with pleasure, sending me over the precipice.

I grabbed my cock and stroked, base to the slick bell. Holding my sides, he growled like a bear pushing deep inside, filling me with his affection. I inhaled sharply, stroking faster and then I groaned loud, a raw sound of immense gratification as my cum hit his chest. The sticky heat webbed my fingers and I tugged a little slower, wanting to prolong the orgasm to the very last, until it hurt.

Sated, I collapsed. Brody eased out, letting me go, falling like a lead weight beside me. We were both sweaty and winded, never-theless content. After a few minutes, he disappeared in the bath-room, returning with a towel and passing it to me. I wiped the mess between my legs.

The bed moved, and he spooned me, hugging my chest. I'd hoped he'd say something, anything. I had wanted to because I was pretty certain we loved each other. But any verbal declaration of affection didn't seem to be in the cards. He kissed the back of my head and I fell asleep in his arms.

~

IN THE MORNING, we discussed what to do next and the decision was unanimous—we had to get away from the city. With the four dead men at the Black Knight, and Gino and his girlfriend at the Regent, someone would eventually put two and two together. After a quick breakfast, we packed clothes, weapons, and stuffed a duffel bag with money.

As Brody zipped the bag, I noticed a sparkle on the windowsill overlooking the main street. I held the black marble to the daylight, fascinated by the heart of vibrant swirling red with only one holographic letter in the center. I froze at the sight of it—everything we'd planned came crashing down in an instant. I squeezed the tiny glass ball and nearly cried. It was sad and wrong how End Life controlled people's lives.

"Hey," I said in a monotone over my shoulder, "I found another marble. It's exactly like the one you have." He snatched it from me and examined it.

"We have to leave immediately." He threw it away and helped put the duffel bag over my shoulders. "An agent of End Life left it here while we were asleep."

"I know. I saw it...the Z. I'm you're next target."

He looked me in the eyes and touched my cheek, giving an affectionate rub. "Don't worry. Didn't I tell you, I'd never hurt you?"

"I'm not worried about you, Brody. What if they send someone else to do it? Maybe that marble was a warning."

"It was, in a way. If I don't kill you, they will send someone else to finish the job."

"But that's crazy! I haven't done anything!"

"I already explained. I want you to take the money and get to the bus station just like we discussed."

"I'm not going anywhere without you. I love you."

"Do you understand what you're saying?"

"I do." I caught hold of his blazer and yanked him close. "So you'd better not ditch me here. Not now! Not ever!"

He abruptly turned, gun drawn, and that's when I saw the intruder, the sliver of a figure near the doorway. I let go of Brody's jacket, and that's when he came to life. He squeezed the trigger and a bullet tore through the man then he aimed to the far left, shoving me away, and the pistol discharged another bullet and another. A blitz erupted. I hit the floor, covering my head. The room was full of men, agents of End Life, and they wanted me dead. I closed my eyes, waiting. Whimpers left my lips—incoherent sputters of dread as various objects in the room exploded.

Men yelled amid additional gunfire.

But I never heard a sound from Brody.

Then silence.

When I finally dared to peek, Brody stood above me, pistol lowered to his side. I slowly got to my feet. Eight dead men surrounded us. Windows had been blown out. Furniture clipped. The place looked like a war zone.

"Do you still love me?" he asked, calm as ever.

I nodded.

"Then leave. More agents will be here any minute."

Tightening my grip on the bag straps, I tried not to cry—my heart was breaking. "Will I see you again?"

"I promise." He kissed me.

THE SECOND HE'D killed the agents, he'd set a series of events in to motion that couldn't be ignored. End Life had invested billions in the Snuff program and it wasn't about to allow their most lucrative asset to walk away.

Three weeks after my bus trip, as per Brody's instructions, I settled in the town of Peardonville, a remote farming community in the south prairie, hundreds of miles from the city. Thanks to a low population and a part-time job, I lived a meager existence. I rented a tiny bachelor suite. It was clean, warm, and private, and located above the grocery store where I worked stocking shelves. And every night I'd wrap myself in an old wool blanket and practice reading by lamplight.

I kept track of Brody's movements through the newspapers. The articles never mentioned him by name, but I knew by each headline and story, he was involved. After numerous unexplained murders throughout the city, starting at the warehouse, End Life had no choice and issued a statement warning the public that a government agent had possibly gone rogue. They did it to protect their own interests, of course.

The government demanded the pharmaceutical company retract the statement, claiming it was false and End Life had no evidence. But rumors of propaganda quickly surfaced and spread, along with abuse of the government's authority, and Brody's brand of justice rose to an almost legendary status. No one had ever heard of the Snuff program, and the public began to demand answers.

In the months to follow, tension grew in the city as word leaked of Brody's past exploits. A list of his targets was given to the newspaper. The public retaliated. The police and anyone viewed as a government worker were openly attacked in the streets. As for me, I remained vigilant, even though my memories had begun to feel more like dreams.

Eighteen months later, Brody still hadn't arrived. I longed for his affection and company, but accepted living alone and, by the two-year mark, I'd given up hope of ever seeing him again. I tried to stay optimistic, but as more time passed, I had to face the inevitable.

During that long, arduous period, I'd accumulated more books and magazines, a box full of throwaways I'd found in dumpsters or recycling bins. I was very proud of myself, as I'd read each one. Just as Brody had told me, my comprehension of the English language, both written and read, improved drastically.

The clock on the bedside table ticked, lulling me to sleep. Someone smoothed my hair, and I opened my eyes. Slowly, Brody came in to focus—dressed in jeans and a bomber jacket—his glasses were gone and his hair unkempt, past his shoulders. It had been so long, I feared his image was an illusion. And yet, I still extended a hand to touch him, my fingertips reaching, and then caressing his stubbly chin. He was living and breathing, flesh and bone, and he had finally returned to me.

"It's really you," I said with softness, shedding several tears.

He cupped my hand to his lips and kissed it, closing his eyes. "I've missed you, Zeus."

His words were the sweetest anyone had ever whispered to me.

MAXIMUM KILL

Book Two

AUTHOR'S NOTE

Kiss the Reaper came to me in a flash—a short story with a plot that could easily be expanded into a series. I envisioned Z first: an unassuming, young male prostitute with a kind heart. Brody emerged from the shadows behind him. He wasn't a solid persona to start, but eventually he took control of my fingers as I typed. By the end of the book, both men had grown on me, Brody in particular. His cold-blooded indifference gave him an indefinable sexual allure. I thought that if I peeled away enough layers, maybe I'd find a little humanity.

Maximum Kill is the second book in my Reaper series, and it's written from three different perspectives. Z is kidnapped, and during the course of his ordeal, he discovers why Brody was given the nickname *the Reaper*. Enjoy!

CHAPTER ONE

he snow was deep. The hard surface crunched, sinking under my boots with each step, and the moisture in my breath misted as soon as it hit the air. Clouds blotched the dreary sky, and the entire landscape was peaceful, sleeping soundlessly under a mantle of white. I'd just finished shopping, and a bag of groceries hung from each hand. I'd lived through some harsh winters in the city, but in the country it was a totally different season, fraught with hardship. Storms blinded, and temperatures frequently dipped below minus fifty. Panting, I trudged through the field and over a section of broken fence, a shortcut home from the grocery store.

Once Brody had eliminated his target—a select group of government officials, the original founders of the Snuff program—his personal vendetta came, in essence, to an end, and we'd moved from Peardonville to a neighboring community three miles away. With one main street and a scattering of dirt side roads, the village of Beisicker had a residual population of ten from its original four hundred—mostly the dispossessed seeking shelter from the authorities. The businesses were boarded up, and vehicles had been left to rot. The village had no running water or power; all amenities had been cut.

So after an extensive search, we'd taken possession of an abandoned, single-room cottage nestled in the outlying forest, minutes from the main street. We cooked and kept warm with a wood burning stove and used oil lamps at night. Luckily there was an old-fashioned hand pump in the backyard. Bath water had to be heated on the stove, so we only bathed a couple of times a week. Dismal as our situation seemed, it wasn't. I thoroughly savored the peace.

Nearly a week previous, Brody had departed without so much as a word. I didn't expect him to tell me what he did outside our relationship. I'd grown accustomed to a certain amount of secrecy. If he felt I needed to know something, he told me; otherwise I didn't ask and feigned ignorance. I couldn't say for certain, but I suspected that his silence was a safety precaution.

I ascended the short flight of snow-covered steps to the front porch. At the top, I grabbed the rail and stopped for a moment to catch my breath. Inside, the dry heat that only a wood fire can produce wafted my frozen cheeks. I'd left the stove on a slow burn to keep the place cozy. Hard bits of snow fell everywhere as I hung my tuque on a hook near the door and unraveled my scarf.

I put the few tinned and dried goods in a cupboard, and the milk and vegetables in a plastic recycling container outside on the narrow, covered veranda at the rear of the cottage. Then for dinner I made Brody's favorite, chicken stir-fry, in the hope I'd surprise him if he happened to walk through the door. But since six days had already passed, I'd begun to think the worst. What if the government had finally caught up with him? Although Brody seemed indestructible, he was still made of flesh and bone.

With my stomach comfortably full, I stared despondently out the living room window, a cigarette dangling between my fingers. Soft wisps of smoke rose in swirls, like delicate lace around an invisible pole. The backyard was a frost bitten jungle. The fire snapped and popped. And the gloomy weather seemed to amplify my depression.

The night before Brody had disappeared, we'd fooled around. I hadn't anticipated a long, heartfelt confession of his undying love, but I had hoped he'd say something. Brody wasn't ardent. He was passionless and direct in everything he said. Every action was calculated. I had learned that much after a year of living with him. He always planned several moves in advance, like a chess player. And he never left anything to chance.

Regardless, I missed him, and I hated to be alone.

Noise at the front of the cottage startled me. Mashing out my cigarette, I looked in the direction of the door. I quickly grabbed the pistol from the top drawer of an ancient hutch next to the stove, and dashed into the kitchen. Looters were rare, since the village had been stripped clean of valuables long before we took up residence. However, squatters and transients weren't. We had to be careful of anyone poking around.

I peered out the window as a pair of scruffy men set a steamer trunk on the porch, their movements muted. Then they rushed back to an old rust bucket of a truck parked on the lane, got in, and drove away. After the pickup disappeared, I slipped on my boots, gripped the gun, and edged onto the porch to investigate. The air frosted my breath and I shivered, giving my arm a rub. I scanned the lane and property. The scuffed, black trunk had a tarnished brass hasp with a padlock, brass hinges, and corner bumpers. Something told me to leave it be.

I hastily went back inside, locking the various chains on the door behind me. Then I stood in the living room, hand on my hip, wondering what to do. The trunk had no labels. No marks. Nothing. Not even a sticker. The whole situation made me nervous. *Who were those men? What's inside the trunk? Why did they leave it?* Just like everything else in my life since I'd met Brody, the trunk and the men who'd left it behind were a mystery. So I decided, right then, that if Brody didn't show up by morning, I'd vacate the cottage and head back to Peardonville.

What am I getting so worked up for? I sighed loudly, and my shoulders drooped; I had bigger worries. I knelt at the wood stove and opened the doors. Orange embers rippled in a dying heat wave that wouldn't sustain me through the night. And the kindling box was empty.

With only a couple of hours of daylight remaining, time was of the essence. I dressed quickly, put on my knapsack, and grabbed the hatchet. I hesitated at the door, then shoved the pistol in my coat pocket and walked to the lane. Eventually, the lane twisted to join with the main road, and I followed it past the field toward a copse and footbridge, which led to a smaller field south of the village. Sunken beyond the reach of daylight, the outlying forest hovered in dreamy grayscale. I'd never gone into the forest—I wasn't adventurous, and the ominous atmosphere put me on edge. I preferred to chop down the young trees and new growth that was slowly reclaiming the clearing.

A rowan had fallen, probably in a storm. It was perfect for burning. Removing the hatchet, I trudged through deeper snow to get closer. I chopped a bough into logs that I put inside the knapsack. After an hour of breaking down several large branches, something moved among the tightly packed trees. I paused and stared unblinking at the spot for the longest time, a murky gloom of incongruous shapes. I had the unnerving sensation that someone or something was watching. My pulse rose, thumping in my ears. Maybe if I didn't look at it, it wouldn't look at me. So I concentrated on my task. I slid my arms through the straps, hiked the knapsack onto my shoulders, and sheathed the hatchet on my belt.

At the base of the hill, I stopped, exhausted and on the verge of collapse. Adjusting the bundle of wood, I gulped at the frigid air and the dry soreness in my throat. Then a shadow emerged from the darkened fringe of forest on my right, and a second figure appeared on my left, followed by another behind the first. Bundled in heavy, camouflage attire and armed with hunting rifles, they weren't looters or squatters but something much worse. The other homeless people in the village talked about survivalists, a group of men who lived beyond society's morality within the deepest part of the forest. They were described as abnormal in appearance, with sallow, twisted features and sunken eyes. An older woman told me that they had abducted one of the homeless men who'd wandered too far from Beisicker, and no one had seen him again. When I asked why they'd taken him, she said she didn't know. So when the three silhouettes came into view, an icy chill trickled down my spine. I didn't bother to ask questions; I turned and ran.

Stumbling and clambering through the snow, I rushed west to get back to the road. *Do they know about the cottage? Have they been watching me? Are they the same men from before?* My mind raced, as did my heart, the fear driving me faster. The bundle of wood, and the fact that I could freeze to death without it, seemed trivial now. The weight was a hindrance, and when I reached the road, I dropped the knapsack. I didn't know where to go. The cottage could be a trap, I was over an hour from civilization, and it was nearly dark.

Anything could happen in the dark.

I bolted in the direction of the village, only to slide to a stop moments later. Six men toting shotguns and rifles were waiting at the far end of the road. I drew sharp breaths. The temperature had plummeted with the fading light, and the air had become bitterly cold. My eyes watered, and I bit the inside of my lower lip; I wanted to cry, and I felt weak in my legs and knees. I nervously looked behind me, and just as I feared, there were more men.

"Who are you?" I wanted to flee and hide. I wished I were one snowflake among gazillions, small and insignificant. "What do you want?"

They slowly closed in, each taking aim. *Why won't they speak?*

"What do you want?" I shouted again, whipping out the pistol Brody had left me. Shaking, I pointed it at them.

Then a gunshot split the eerie silence like a crack of lightning, echoing off the surrounding buildings and forest, and the side of one man's head exploded. Startled, I ducked. The dead man fell to the ground, and red soaked through the snow—a creeping river of red. The others hollered at each other and dashed for cover just as a second shot rang through the ice-cold atmosphere. Another guy close to me tumbled into a ditch. The men returned fire. I quickly crawled for the field and dove behind an embankment. I recognized the distinctive sound of one gun among the others: the short, powerful burst of an M9.

The battle continued for several minutes. Bullets whizzed past and walloped the snow. And men emitted cries of pain. Then Beisicker was once again tranquil. I was about to look over the bank when the snow crunched on the other side. Someone was approaching.

I squeezed my eyes shut. *Please don't find me. Please—*

Someone grabbed my hood and I yelled, scrambling to get away.

"It's me."

At the sight of Brody bundled in a ski jacket, scarf, and gloves, pistol in hand, I almost burst in to tears.

He crouched next to me. "Did they hurt you?"

"Nearly!" I pressed a fist into the snow.

"Nearly isn't a definitive answer," he said in a soft voice, looking me straight in the eyes.

After inhaling deeply a few times, I calmed. "Not nearly, but I'm pretty sure they wanted to. Whatever. I'm fine."

He helped me to my feet, and to my surprise wrapped me in a strong embrace. "I should've come sooner. Forgive me."

It was odd for him to apologize. Maybe he genuinely felt bad. Regardless, the warmth of his breath on my forehead immediately eased the stress, and I buried my face in his jacket and hugged him tightly. I wanted to call him a jerk and nail his ass to the wall for taking too fucking long to return. But I couldn't do it.

"I assume everyone's dead." I let go and passed him my gun.

"You assume correctly." He removed the empty magazine, took a full one from his jacket pocket, and shoved it into the butt before giving it back to me.

"In my rush, I forgot to reload it... Sorry."

"In the face of evil, a gun devoid of bullets is like a priest without his Bible: powerless."

"Nice analogy," I mumbled defiantly.

"It wasn't meant to be *nice*."

"I know... It was a stupid thing to do. But I kind of panicked."

"Not stupid, however foolhardy. You must learn self-restraint. Slow down, and think."

We left the field. Twilight had settled around us, and we were submerged in the soft refraction and scattering of the sun's rays. Objects blended into the backdrop of greenery, including Brody's dark clothes as he walked ahead. Near the footbridge, he retrieved my frozen knapsack and hatchet.

On the way back to the cottage, I explained about the steamer trunk, the scruffy men, and my trip to gather firewood. We tramped up the porch steps; the trunk was exactly where the men had left it. He shot the padlock, then used his boot to tip the lid. Inside were a roll of duct tape, plastic bags, and a heavy, fibrous rope, all common tools for kidnapping.

"What the hell...?" I examined the roll of tape.

"They had planned to take you during the night."

I stood up. "You're telling me they would've stuffed me inside this thing?"

"Yes. A perfect means of concealed transport."

"There's no way. I'm too big. They would've had to break my limbs."

"A minor drawback."

Confused, I followed him inside the cottage. "What are you implying?"

He set the knapsack of kindling on the floor and unzipped his ski jacket. "There were eleven people in the village when we arrived. Less than a week later, there were ten. The day the eleventh person disappeared, I discovered two additional sets of footprints in the snow outside the building where he lived. The implications are obvious."

"So the old lady was right. Someone else had been there." I knelt beside him as he set pieces of kindling inside the wood stove.

"The question is *who*."

"That's why you left me here."

"Three days later, I caught the same men watching this cottage."

I shuddered at the news. "That's kind of stalker-ish. Why didn't you tell me?"

"Normalcy was paramount."

"In other words, you used me as bait." My chest tightened at the thought; I felt betrayed, even though I understood why he'd done it.

"Unfortunately, it was the only option. Once I realized what they were after, I needed to know how many I was dealing with."

"Not to sound like an idiot, but I don't get it. I mean...what did those guys want with me? Sex—or what?"

"I can't guarantee there wouldn't have been some type of ritualistic hedonism if they'd captured you. However, that wasn't their real agenda. They were cannibals, Zeus," Brody said evenly, his gaze entranced by the growing fire. "They'd planned to make you their next meal."

Holy crap. My mouth instantly began to salivate, and I rubbed at the queasy twinge knotting my stomach. I was about to ask how he knew, but apparently he'd read my mind.

"Human skeletal remains littered a shallow grave near their encampment."

"You shouldn't have followed them...not alone, anyway."

"Needs must when the devil drives." He blinked and stared at me, flames dancing in the steely sheen of his gaze. "And you are such an attractive devil."

He touched my chin and smoothed my bottom lip with his thumb. Then he kissed me. Heat scored my cheeks and I felt like a blushing schoolgirl. We were lovers, and he'd seen me at my very best and very worst, but somehow I still got embarrassed when he said anything tenuously affectionate.

"What happens now?"

"We leave in the morning."

I wasn't thrilled with the prospect of moving again. I'd grown accustomed to the cottage and enjoyed living our private, simple existence. But Brody explained that the men he'd killed had come from an encampment in the mountains. He wasn't certain of their exact numbers.

I readily agreed to leave first thing.

CHAPTER TWO

e departed at first light with what little we owned slung over our backs and boarded a bus in Peardonville. Our destination was a small town called Rosedale, eight hours away and four hundred and thirty-four miles southeast of Beisicker.

With my cheek stuck to the window I watched the scenery pass, cataloging the landmarks and places I didn't recognize. The winter months were boring, a monochrome terrain tainted by the cold. Brody slept beside me then read a physics textbook. At one of the rest stops we got off the bus to stretch. We dined on prepackaged, convenience store meals. I was peeling open a ham and cheese on rye when out of the blue Brody began to talk.

"My father was a neurosurgeon and my mother was a doll maker."

I set down my sandwich without taking a bite. "Doll maker... that's an odd profession. What kind of dolls?"

"Collectibles. Her handmade porcelain creations were displayed in galleries from coast to coast."

I thought about what it must've been like to live with such intelligent and gifted parents. My mother had bordered on brainless, thanks to years of heavy drug use. "So, your family had status and wealth."

"In the conventional sense."

"Where are they now?"

Brody tore the plastic wrap on a Caesar salad. "My mother was killed in a car accident, and my father's a recluse."

"Do you ever visit him?"

"Never." He set the bowl on his tray. "What about your father?"

He'd never taken the initiative—never asked about my life—and I actually got excited, despite the fact that my personal history wasn't worth sharing.

"I never knew him, but I knew who he was, because my mother pointed him out once. What the hell for, I don't know."

"Posterity."

"Maybe." I clasped both hands behind my head. "He had brown hair and eyes and plain features. He was just this average guy with a thing for hookers."

"Penchant for the perverse."

"Something like that." I chuckled and finished eating my food.

He chewed on lettuce, swallowed, then said, "I had a twin. He died shortly after our birth."

I was stunned. Honestly, I couldn't fathom Brody with a family, though he obviously had parents like everyone else. "Were they cruel to you?"

He turned his face to the side and grinned, searching my expression. "Contrary to what popular science would have the world believe, I'm not who I am due to childhood trauma. My parents were normal. Very attentive, very doting."

"I never meant to assume anything..." I sighed. "Ah, shit. I'm sorry."

"I've told you numerous times. There is no need for you to apologize, ever. You can speak your mind. Ask me anything."

"Are you sure...?"

"You aren't deaf, Zeus."

"I just want to make certain." I leaned close to him and whispered discreetly, "When we get to wherever we're going, can we do it?"

After a moment of what seemed like quiet reflection, he put down his plastic fork and caught my gaze dead center. Desire smoldered in the depths of his, and I was instantly aroused. "Sex with you is the best."

Another hour of gloomy skyline and white, lifeless countryside passed my line of sight. We sailed through city, suburbia, and farmland, town after town, until the bus slowed and turned onto an industrial road. The brakes screeched, and I straightened, wiping the condensation from the window as the driver announced that we'd reached Rosedale. Our final destination was a rundown horseshoe of motel units half a mile off the highway at the outskirts of the town, a place where the majority of customers were truck drivers. I didn't care where we stayed as long as it was warm and dry with a double bed.

We waited our turn to exit, filing out last after a pair of giggling teenage girls. I followed Brody to the motel office. He checked us in under an alias and got the key. Ours was a unit in the east section.

"How far are we from the town?"

"Minutes. The main street is directly behind the motel." He unlocked the deadbolt and shoved the door.

I let my knapsack slough to the floor. The double-occupancy room had a queen-size bed, lamps, a table and pair of chairs, and a nasty-ass shag carpet in tri-tone gold. Even the TV was archaic and coated in a decade of dust. The air smelled musty. However, for two fugitives on the run, the place was adequate.

"I'm going to shower." I dropped my coat over a chair. "I need to warm up."

I pressed on the pinkish-beige tile as the water spilled over my head and shoulders. The heat felt good, and I scrubbed at my scalp. In Brody's absence, I'd gone days at the cottage without bathing, because it was too much of a hassle. So I savored the warmth. I tightened the taps and droplets fell from the showerhead. I heard the slight vibration of canned laughter; the TV was on. I dried myself and hung the towel. There wasn't any point in covering myself when we were going to fuck. As I grabbed the knob I paused for a moment, suddenly self-conscious. *This is stupid. He's seen me naked before.* Finally, I threw caution into the wind. I opened and shut the door to find Brody lying under the covers, flicking through the channels.

"Intellectual programming doesn't exist."

"I don't think it ever has...nothing that would be to your standard, anyway."

He grinned and set the remote on the nightstand. "I can smell shampoo from here."

"Yeah, I guess...better than sweat." I crawled in beside him.

He got close and we kissed, slow and fervent, before he fisted my hair and forced my head back. He held my chin and his tongue mingled with mine. Then he eased away, his lips wet with saliva, and I exhaled a wisp of a sigh. The kiss had been life draining. And my lips tingled. I'd never felt that kind of intensity from him before. Maybe his feelings for me had grown. I wanted to ask, but soon forgot as he moved lower, caressing my throat and chest while gently gripping my sides. Brody had strong hands—long, wiry fingers that felt incredible raking my flesh. He lightly traced the curve of my spine to my buttocks and nuzzled the base of my cock.

"Get on your hands and knees."

I didn't care for doggie style. It was a shameful position that many men had used to take advantage of me. But I was dying for his affection and got on all fours. He spread my ass and dragged his tongue over my opening like a dog would lap water; I squeezed my eyes shut and fisted the bedding. He'd never rimmed me. My heart started to pound and a feverish dampness rose across my upper lip. "Agh... This position is..." I tried to move, but he exerted just enough strength that I couldn't.

"I won't hurt you," he said softly. I froze. Once again he'd read my mind, sensed my distress. "I've always wanted to taste you, Zeus. Will you let me?"

Holy shit. I felt faint; he'd never talked to me that way. "Yeah, I'll let you."

He held my pelvis steady and thoroughly got a taste. My cock hung with a slight rigid arc and I backed my ass into his face; I wanted him to fuck me so bad. But when I peered over my shoulder, he was sitting on his ankles, knees bent.

"Straddle my lap."

With my legs spread, I carefully sat on his lap, and he clamped his left arm across my chest and held my jaw with his right hand. It was a strange position: if he let go, I'd fall flat on my face. But as he lifted his hips, his cock slid in deep, and I expelled a loud grunt. Pinching my jaw, he nibbled my ear. "Masturbate for me."

What the hell's got into him? "O-okay..." Embarrassed, I closed my eyes and grabbed my dick. As I stroked, adding a little extra pressure to the slick head, he kissed the side of my face, and we were unexpectedly in sync. His thrusts and my strokes were perfectly matched.

"That's it," he encouraged, his hot breath warm on my nape.

I forgot where we were; my mind had gone blank, and the feeling had taken control. He let go of my jaw and grabbed my hand, pressing his fingers between mine and helping me masturbate with more vigor. We groaned, and in a blinding flash, we both came. The milky heat shot from my cock. He slowly released my torso and I planted my hands and knees on the bed before collapsing onto my side. Panting, Brody stared at the ceiling with a satisfied expression, his arms dangling at his sides.

"Was it good?" I immediately felt like an idiot for asking. Even lousy sex could feel good.

He looked at me. "Needless worry will make you ill."

"I'm not... I..." I sighed, rolled onto my back, and bent an arm over my eyes.

"You overanalyze. Haven't I already told you that sex with you is the best?"

"I know you have, but that's not the point. The point is, we're supposed to be lovers, and when two people are lovers they usually —" I stopped mid-sentence. There was no use in explaining the difference between the physical act of sex and making love to a man who lacked basic emotional attachment. He was too intelligent not to understand the mechanics of it, and I was the only one who'd get hurt. I had to remind myself whom I'd fallen in love with. Brody was a killer. He had a disparate thought process, and I was positive whatever he felt for me would never match what I felt for him. "Never mind." I got up and sat on the edge of the mattress. "Are you going to shower? Because I need another one."

He searched my face as if he wanted to tell me something. But then he said evenly, "You can go first."

I examined my overall appearance in the mirror: pallid complexion, ribs protruding. All I could see was a weak and frail man. Maybe that's why Brody stuck around: I was easy prey. I shaved, showered, then put on a T-shirt and underwear.

The only show that came in clearly on the TV was some nature program. I dropped the remote on the bed and lit a cigarette as a lion chased a hyena across the Serengeti.

The bathroom door opened, and Brody wandered out, drying himself.

"If you could have any animal as pet, which would you choose?"

With a quizzical expression, he pulled on a pair of sweats. "A wolverine."

I smirked, tapping ash into the ashtray. "That is *so* you."

"It is." He grinned, rubbing the side of his head.

Brody had described himself perfectly. He was a fearless loner with a ferocious violent streak, especially when cornered—a creature that would take on anyone and anything. And the only time he was physically approachable was when it came to sex.

CHAPTER THREE

The marble glistened in the sunlight—one inch of neon purple interwoven with solid black, a sphere of death. Maxine held it higher between nails coated in purple varnish. The holographic letters shimmered. After looking intently at the glass orb for a while, she tucked it inside a jacket pocket and patted the small lump for good measure. Then she made her way down a flight of steep, icy steps, her gloved hand sliding along a guardrail of pitted black paint. At the bottom was a steel door. She knocked, and a slot near the top shot open. A pair of dark eyes, shaded by a dense brow line, peered out.

"Password?" a man asked.

How cliché. "Raspberry jam," she replied sweetly, twirling the end of her right pigtail around a finger.

Bolts were pulled, metal scraped, and the door permitted her entry.

"Thanks." She flashed the hulking guard a coy smile and wiggled her fingers at him before disappearing in a narrow passageway.

The passage gradually descended into 'the pit,' a subterranean coliseum of bleachers filled to its maximum capacity of four hundred. The air was suffocating. Spectators waved bidding slips in their faces in an attempt to fan away the unbearable humidity. Pit fighting was an illegally sponsored sport. But that didn't stop big bets from floating around.

Dressed like a modernized Spartan warrior, Mad Dog, the reigning champion two years in a row, curled his arms at his chest like a pro wrestler. At six feet eight, he was stacked, with exaggerated muscles and thighs as wide as tree trunks. He wore the silver bands of a contract fighter on his wrists and upper arms, and his chest was branded with a large tattoo of shredded wings on a cross bound in barbed wire.

He was led by his sponsor, a diminutive, green-eyed redhead who tugged on a chain, causing the leather dog collar to bite into his neck. The metal staircase shook as he stepped down, and he walked bow-legged into the center of the ring—a dirt floor outlined in white chalk. The crowd went wild with hoots and jeers, encouraging him, their fighter of choice.

She knew the monstrosity belonged to the redhead, and the woman rarely left his side. "I've heard if he isn't kept restrained, he goes berserk. You've got to appreciate a man like that." Maxine slapped a banded wad of bills on the betting table.

The cashier snatched the cash, licked his thumb, and started to count. "Haven't seen you in a long time."

"Been busy. It's all there."

"Rules are rules, darlin'," he said with a twang. "And I don't make 'em."

"Understood." She waited, one hand on her thin waist, watching like a hawk as he divided the bills into groups of a thousand while keeping a wary eye on the pit.

"Ten thousand." The cashier nudged the bookie, and a grungy four-eyed kid wrote in a black ledger.

"Sign here." He slid the book around and pointed a gritty fingernail at the faded blue line beside her name and wager.

She signed, got her bidding slip, and walked away from the table. The line of eager bidders moved forwards by a foot. Angling past the spectators, she climbed several levels to sit on a top bleacher.

Within the hour, all final bets were taken and the fighting commenced. Although illegal, the sport was organized. Similar to boxing, all the combatants were placed into a weight class: flyweight, lightweight, welterweight, and heavyweight. Size and mass meant everything in the ring, even the difference between life and death. And it was that sheer brutality that Maxine found too irresistible to resist. The only rules were no biting, no verbal coercion, and no shots to the groin. If a fighter broke the rules, he was banned.

When the last pair of heavyweights—Mad Dog and a relatively new fighter, Shingo—entered the pit, her focus became grounded. She removed the marble from her pocket and reexamined it. Then her gaze drifted to the target. He was a big sucker, the biggest she'd ever had to take down.

The match was brutally swift, lasting less than ten minutes. She watched, entranced, as Mad Dog crushed his opponent against the metal guardrail and then knocked him out cold with a shot to the face. Victorious, he yelled at the crowd and flexed his arms to a mix of cheers and boos. The losing bidders threw their slips into the air.

Putting the marble back into her pocket, she descended the bleachers and collected her winnings. Near the change room entrance, she leaned against the wall in a casual manner. Mad Dog approached. She batted her long lashes, drinking in his male prowess, and ran her fingers up her bare thigh to her miniskirt, where she pawed at the material, revealing the lacy seam of her panties. He grunted and pivoted his head right then left, cracking his neck. There wasn't any need for words; the hunger was evident in his dark eyes.

Outside, they stumbled into a brick wall, the perimeter of an old ice cream factory that concealed the pit. The air was crisp, and a low-hanging overhead lamp illuminated their silhouettes. He grabbed the scruff of her jacket and yanked her close. She moaned, pushing at his arms, but he devoured her breath and saliva then roughly kissed her chin and throat. She gasped. He was too strong. She couldn't break free.

"Enough of the sweet shit." He got a fistful of her pigtail, abruptly turned her in the opposite direction, and slammed her into the wall. "Now you're gonna do what I want, bitch."

She pressed her palms on the brick, sucking in the cold; the jagged edges of mortar were rough and scraped her fingertips. "Okay, yeah, I'll do whatever you say."

He lifted her skirt and tore her panties; the delicate elastic band snapped her bare butt. He unzipped his fly and pushed against her, nudging the back of her thighs with his cock. The penetration shocked; she gasped and rose slightly on the balls of her feet.

She glared at the frosted brick as their skin slapped and he grunted like a pig with each thrust. She leaned backward and tried get her nails into his neck, but couldn't. Then she remembered why she was there, why she'd lured him to a secluded spot. The man would, in a moment be no more, a figment of her past and a corpse that the public would never miss. Reaching inside her blazer, she touched the hard plastic grip of the knife. Whipped it out and drove it into his leg. He swore, pushing away from her, and then she turned and sunk the steel deep between his ribs. "You fucking bitch!" He hit her, and she fell into the wall. But she quickly scooped the knife from the ground and planted it in his chest a second time. No matter his size and strength, his delicate human flesh couldn't stop the blade.

Gradually, he sank to his knees, clutching his side.

She watched with mild curiosity as the man at her feet struggled to breathe. The puncture holes frothed scarlet bubbles as life-giving oxygen poured forth. He landed face down on the pavement, his limbs deflating like a flattened tire. She wiped her mouth with the back of her hand and dropped to squat over his back. Lifting his head by the hair, she reached under his jowl and cut his throat.

He sputtered if for a split second, the final attempt at survival then lay motionless, like a beached whale.

The deed was done. The target had been eliminated. She wiped the ten-inch hunting blade on his clothes. Concealed it inside her blazer, and picked up her tattered underwear. Then she straightened her skirt and exited the alley to the hustle and bustle of a busy Friday night in the city.

Back at home, she found sanctuary. She stripped and stepped inside the shower. The water steamed, filling the cubicle and washed away the disgusting reek of male bodily fluids—the sweat and sex. Men were pigs. Users. Abusers. And she hated them all.

Later, seated on the bed, she dried her purple hair, then combed and retied it into two long pigtails.

In the morning, she awoke to find another marble inside her mailbox. She ate and got dressed. Exited her apartment and locked the door. Jogged a short flight of steps, pigtails bouncing, and crossed the street. Walked east four city blocks, slipped inside a public phone booth, and shut the door. Plugged several coins in the slot and pressed a string of numbers followed by the number sign. The line rang twice then clicked.

"Yes...?" a man with a German accent answered.

"It's me."

"Are you speaking from the secure line?"

"391 in the heart of the city." She watched intently as a few drops of rain quickly transformed into a torrential downpour.

"Good. What about the subject?"

"It's done."

"Excellent."

"Oh, and I don't know what's happening, but I received a second marker." Nuzzling the receiver against her shoulder, she studied the purple and black marble with increasing concern. "The name inside is a fellow inmate."

"That's correct."

"What happened? Did he disrupt your plans again?" She smirked. "Shit in the wrong sandbox?"

After a moment, the man replied, "He quit taking his medication and declared himself healed."

"I supposed that kind of shit happens when the prodigal son is allowed to run amok." She frowned, squeezing the marble; rain pebbled the booth, distorting a streetlamp and pedestrians rushing along the sidewalk. "It won't be easy. He isn't exactly a newbie. He's more like the grand master."

The man laughed quietly in a patronizing sort-of-way. "What exactly is it that scares you? The fact that he's extremely good at what he does, or the fact that you, once again, feel inferior?"

"I'm not scared of anyone, and inferiority is simply a state of mind."

"Then you should have no problem. His last known whereabouts was the village of Beisicker. Kill him, or you will wind up in a similar predicament."

The line went dead.

She lingered for a moment, glaring at the receiver; the man had audacity to speak to her like that. Enraged, she slammed it on the hook several times in a frenzied attack. "Stupid old fucker! If it wasn't for me, you'd be up shit creek without a paddle!" She banged the phone one last time, opened the accordion door, cinched her snug-fitting blazer at her throat, and stepped into the freezing rain.

Back inside her apartment, she secured all the locks and chains and marched into the living room. The bleak daylight gave the patio curtains a dull but eerie glow. "Shit. Fuck. Shit—fuck!" She whipped her soaked jacket at the couch. "Why me? Lard ass should do it!"

She didn't want to fight one of her own, especially Brody. Brody was different, and she feared a less than optimal outcome. During training, she'd overheard the hushed conversations between various pharmaceutical personnel. Brody was exceptional, one of a kind, flawless—a natural born killer with an extraordinary set of skills and near-superhuman abilities. He never trained, not like her and Jack. His superior intelligence made it easy for him to adapt to any opponent, and that's what set him apart. Brody was what Doctor Günter had described as a 'mimic.'

Frustrated, she grabbed both pigtails and pulled on them until they were straight. She needed to take her mind off the forthcoming days. She stood in front of the second bedroom, feeling for the key jammed behind the trim casing, then she unlocked the door. Inside, she flicked the light switch. A young man, gagged, his wrists and ankles tied to the bedposts, squinted against the harsh brightness. As soon as he saw her, a tear ran from the corner of his eye. He'd been lying naked in the same spot for days, and the rope had scored deep into his flesh from his struggling.

She sat next to him and the mattress bounced. Walking two fingers up his sinewy thigh, she exhaled a mournful sigh. "Have you missed me, baby?"

His chin quivered and he squeezed his eyes shut.

"It stinks in here. Looks like you pissed yourself again. I suppose you'll need another enema too. Then I've got to change the sheets." He mumbled loudly, and she removed the gag from his mouth. "What did you say?"

"Sh-shower, please... I'd rather have a...show-wer."

"I suppose, but you aren't going in alone."

After she'd assisted him in the shower, she wrapped him in a terry cloth robe then set a plate of cold fries and a burger on the kitchen table. He only resisted the food for a few seconds before succumbing to his hunger. Once he'd finished, she forcibly walked him back into his prison.

"Please don't tie me up."

"I won't be long."

"What?" He panicked, and his voice rose in pitch. "What if there's a fire? I'm scared! Don't leave me here like this!"

She put a clean gag in his mouth and knotted it to the back of his head. "If you weren't so damned deceitful, I'd leave you untied. But we both know what happened last time."

He groaned loudly, wiggling and yanking on the rope as she shut the door.

~

WIPERS SWISHING, the car rolled slowly past a dilapidated gas station–slash–truck stop. She put the shifter in park and opened the driver's side with a whoosh. Bitterly cold winds billowed her short skirt. Shading her eyes, she surveyed the village. A pock-marked sign with black letters read *Beisicker—Unincorporated*. It didn't take her long to detect Brody's handiwork: nine dead men half-buried in snowdrifts. The village was a cemetery. She ran back to the car and hopped inside. Cranked the heat and put her hands over the vents.

She skimmed a mental list of Brody's behavior, his likes and dislikes. She knew his personality would dictate his next destination. Clever or not, he was just like everyone else: transparent. He was a creature of habit. And bad habits were always the hardest to break.

CHAPTER FOUR

*B*rody adjusted his tie in the mirror screwed to the bathroom door, zipped his ski jacket, and sat on the edge of the bed, his arms resting in his lap. He noted the peacefulness of his lover's features in the dusty morning light. He wanted to touch Zeus's hair, but traced the rough stubble along his jaw instead. *Is this an appropriate gesture of affection?* He knew Zeus had been disappointed with his lack of verbal affection the night before and had distanced himself accordingly. He wondered why Zeus stayed. Love was an ambiguous term, and it didn't accurately explicate his feelings for the former prostitute. But then he couldn't understand his own need for the man, nor could he think of any other word more suitable.

"Where are you going so early?" Zeus hugged his pillow and eyed him groggily.

"Into town."

"I can help with the shopping."

"There's no need." He got up. "I'll return shortly."

"Okay."

At the corner of Dunbar and Thurlow, Brody entered a convenience-store to the jangle of teeny-tiny bells. Wisps of snow trailed his strides, blowing across the threshold. Stale air hit his nose first, followed by the overpowering floral scent of perfumed laundry products and dish soap. No matter where he went, people's need to submerge themselves in sickly-sweet odors was an assault to his senses. His gaze absorbed the brightly colored labels. He saw everything in increments, like stills through a camera lens—flashes of objects identified and categorized by shape, size, color, texture, or smell. He dragged his fingers lightly over the different boxes and bottles. Each item produced a unique stimulus, and that information came as a flood washing through his senses to his brain.

"Is there something I can help you find?"

Brody acknowledged the store clerk, making expeditious calculations: *mid-fifties, obese, trouble breathing, approximately five-feet-five, heart attack material and would in all probability die with a hard shot to the chest. No sufficient reason to kill.* He set a slender foil box of strawberry-flavored condoms, two bottles of pop, and a bag of red licorice on the counter. "One pack of Armand Lights."

"Sure." The man reached into a drawer below the lottery machine and put a pack of cigarettes in the bag. "That'll be thirty-five bucks."

He passed the shop owner two twenties, got his change, and grabbed the bag. The bells jangled again as the entrance shut behind him. With each step he was bombarded by more stimuli— other pedestrians, the weather, traffic. Then, when he'd had enough, he shut off the absorption like a faucet. Not a drop of thought got in, and nothing got out. Silence floated inside his head.

As far back as he could recall, he'd had the ability to shut out the world, to see only what he wanted to see, to pick and choose. And when he chose to kill, he enacted the murder in his head, planning for inconsistencies, unforeseen problems, or possible errors in his judgment. Once satisfied that he'd accounted for all variables, he executed with precision timing.

His gaze shifted, instantly drawn to shouting outside of a Laundromat; a couple was in the middle of a heated argument. Observant as ever, he calmly took note and sauntered past. The woman said she'd had enough of the man's cheating. She said they were through, and he backhanded her, sending her sprawling across the ground along with a basket of neatly folded clothes. She wept, holding her mouth as the man yelled above her, berating and threatening. Not one passerby took notice of the couple's abusive tête-à-tête. It never ceased to surprise him how emotionally detached the average person could be.

He blinked slowly, allowing the external stimuli to flow: *young male, athletic build, thirties, with a chip on his shoulder, buildings on either side, six vehicles, multiple escape routes, only one practical, weather perfect to mask noise and decrease the possibility of identification.* He proceeded past the front of the Laundromat and disappeared in an alley. As he walked, he knotted his plastic bag of items and tossed it away behind a dumpster. Reaching inside his jacket, he curled his fingers around the grip of his favorite piece. He exited onto a back street and into blowing snow, a blizzard that somehow encapsulated the immediate area in a dead calm. The man was beating the woman next to a cream SUV. Propped against the front quarter panel, bleeding, the woman put her arms up in defense as the man kneed her.

She looked at Brody then, tears streaming down her bloated face. He read the fear in her watery eyes, eyes that were pleading in desperation. The pain reminded him of Zeus.

Exhaling white, he grimaced and took aim. "I despise cowards."

At the sound of Brody's voice, the man spun around. "Who the hell are you?"

"The Reaper." He squeezed the trigger. The firing pin clicked. And a bullet drilled a hole into the man's chest, snapping his torso back and throwing him onto the icy pavement.

Brody took a moment to soak in the beauty of his handiwork, blood pooling on a stark canvas of the purest white. He loomed above his choking victim like a vulture over a carcass, his mind racing, hundreds of frames of contemplation per second—a gruesome mishmash of those he'd killed and those he'd saved—the rush filling his soul with blinding rage, lust, and near-transcendent gratification. The man beseeched for his life. But those quick to seek mercy after committing a heinous act only fueled his need to cleanse. Crouching, he grabbed the guy by the scruff of his jacket and shot him in the forehead.

"Thank you," the woman murmured, peace easing her disfigured face, and she cracked a lopsided smile.

Holstering the M9, he retraced his steps to the alley, where he retrieved the white plastic bag and headed back to the main road. Five blocks later, he heard sirens wail in the distance.

When he was only a few feet from his motel unit, he stopped. Something was amiss. The door was partly open. He carefully set the bag against the outer wall, drew his gun, and prodded the door. The hinges creaked, and he noted the abnormal silence within and the absence of fresh cigarette smoke.

A chair was overturned, a lamp was on the floor, and the table had been moved. The local news broadcaster was saying that the temperature would plunge overnight.

There'd been a struggle.

Then he saw something too vibrant to belong to Zeus. His lover was a boring man, satisfied with the mundane in life, and he certainly wouldn't wear such a gaudy article of clothing. He loosened the purple scarf from the bathroom doorknob; it stunk of a cheap whore's perfume. *Your slut is mine* was smeared in violet lipstick across the mirror.

The scarf told him two things: End Life had found them. And they'd sent a professional.

He frowned, scrunching it in his fist.

Bait.

Fucking bitch.

CHAPTER FIVE

I turned my head to the side, and it throbbed. Daylight streamed from holes in a green tarpaulin, brittle and smeared in dirt. I put my hand up in defense against the blinding onslaught. I had no idea where I was or how I'd got there. Getting into an upright position, I examined my surroundings; I'd been lying on a bed of canvas and rope. The space was vast, with walls and floor of solid concrete. Square columns held the twenty-foot ceiling struts. I was in a warehouse of some kind, but one that had been in disuse for many years.

The tarp ruffled, flapping high, and a chilly breeze hit my face. Pushing it aside, I found a huge window with broken panes, one of many, that faced an industrial distribution yard overrun with vegetation.

"Oh. The little prince is finally awake."

I jumped, my heart banging my chest to pieces, and stared at what appeared to be a teenage girl with shoulder-length, neon purple pigtails. "Who-o are you? And where am I?"

"Do you always stutter?"

"I'm just nervous...right now."

"Ah, yeah, I know the feeling." She leaned back on a support column, folding her arms. "It sucks when someone else has you by the short and curlies. My name's Maxine. I work for End Life, and you, my little prince, are in an abandoned metal fabrication plant."

"How did I get here?"

"After I knocked you out, I paid a couple of thugs I know to haul your ass to my car. Then we came here, so you could sleep off the effects of the drug, and so we'd have complete privacy."

Clad in a short plaid skirt and a matching neon purple, tartan blazer with black lapels, chewing gum, she looked like an anime schoolgirl, not a professional hit woman. And the boots gave her a sluttish appeal—they were the same shade of purple in leather zipped to mid-thigh. Her cellulite bulged faintly at the seam, and the platinum stiletto heels glistened in the light.

She passed me and sat on a chair, anchoring her elbows over the backrest and crossing her legs. I caught the outline of her snow-white panties.

"Whatcha lookin' at?"

"Nothing." I cleared my throat, diverting my gaze.

"Have a seat." She motioned to a stool covered in dust beside a drafting table, and I sat. "I bet you're just awed because you've never seen such a hot babe before." She circled her foot, bouncing her top leg. "You don't talk much, huh? Brody must like 'em quiet."

We stared at one another for an extended period—me rigid, and her soaking it all in like she was on vacation in the tropics. Then she tossed something at me and I fumbled to catch it. The marker was purple and black, the same as her garish ensemble. The holographic name sent a shudder up my spine.

"You know what that is, right?"

"Yeah," I whispered grimly.

"Good. Then you know I ain't gonna play gentle."

I fisted the marble and looked at her. I wanted to wipe that fatuous smile off her face. Cocky bitch.

"I could never have a lover like Brody has you. Men are inherent cheaters. For instance, my last boyfriend... I caught him in bed with this whore. So I lost it. You know how it is. I saw his cock in her twat, and *bam*! My temper, like, exploded." I nodded in sympathy and she continued to chew the bubble gum. "I stabbed him over and over. And the whore was underneath him—she wouldn't stop screamin' and screamin'—right friggin' pain in my ass she was, so I had to slit her throat too." She made a cutting motion, running two stiff fingers, nails glossy, across her own throat.

"I bet that was annoying," I said.

"Yeah, I know, right?" She wore a quirky grin, like the story was somehow amusing, and then she said between chewing her cud, "Fucking shame it was...fucking shame. But he had to be taught a lesson. Cheaters never prosper. I dismembered them both. Wrapped 'em up in plastic bags like Christmas presents, and tossed 'em out with the trash." She fanned her flushed face with both hands; I assumed the memories were too rousing to handle. "And then I felt better, you know? Like a weight had been lifted from my shoulders."

A rancid taste seared the back of my throat. I swallowed the burn, wishing I had a glass of water and hoping Brody would find us fast; the psycho bitch was making me extremely anxious.

"Sometimes I orgasm when I do it. Now that's a rush!" She hugged her waist giggling.

Temptation lay inches from my grasp on the drafting table. I felt inclined to drive the rusted tin snips into her chest. It was the first time I'd ever felt such a powerful urge to hurt anyone. But then suddenly, she stood in front of me, leaned over, and picked up the snips.

My blood ran cold.

"I know what you're thinkin'." She searched my clammy features, holding them to the light. "You're thinkin', *if I could just grow the balls to do it*. But sadly, you're normal. You have a conscience. You have to contemplate and worry. You need to justify what must be done. You can't just pick these up and," she paused to look at them, "stab me. Even if you were angry enough, you still couldn't do it. Do you know why?"

"No."

Smugly, as if it were the most obvious thing in the world, she said, "Because it isn't in your nature. You're a sad little man who's been abused all his life. People like you never fight back. People like you never rise to the top. People like you are here for the benefit of people like me."

"Who cares if I don't like killing?" I scowled. "That just makes me more human than you."

She got closer, so close the heat of her lips brushed my cheek. "Brody likes to kill," she purred at my earlobe. "So what does that make him?"

"You're a rotten bitch!"

"Make no mistake, little prince. Your lover is the biggest and baddest monster of all." She shoved the tin snips in my face. "Now get the fuck up!"

NEWCOMB WAS a dirty blotch on the horizon like a permanent stain set in a silk blouse—a city surrounded by big skies and hectares of farmland—an overpopulated cesspool in the middle of nowhere. And Maxine's apartment was smack dab in the heart of it.

She parked in the secure underground parking lot then dragged me into the elevator. Her place was spacious: several thousand square feet of penthouse.

By the third night of my captivity, I'd seen her unlock the door to the second room twice. But as I stood in front of it I hesitated, squeezing the key. Not moments before I'd been gung-ho—determined to discover what secrets, if any, lay hidden inside. But my mind strayed. She'd mentioned that she'd dismembered her ex and the girl he was screwing. The thought made me nauseous. So I was almost scared to go any further. What would I find inside the room?

Holding my breath, I shoved the key in and turned the knob,

and the locking mechanism clicked. I froze when I saw a young, naked man lying on the bed. His muffled yelling startled me. I quickly loosened the gag from his mouth.

"Please, help me—please!"

"I can't even help myself," I said, untying his wrists next. "There are double-barreled deadbolts on the front door, and all the windows have bars. This place is like a prison."

"We have to get out."

A thousand questions ran through my mind. "How long have you been here?"

"I don't know... Weeks, I think."

I helped him unbind his ankles. The flesh was rubbed raw. "You have open sores. You need to see a doctor."

His eyes welled up. "The only thing I need is to get out of here. You have no idea what she does to me!"

"Sorry, but after everything I've seen so far, it would be a stupid move."

He hung his head, and tears rolled off his cheeks. "She rapes me and makes me fuck her and beats me... She says it's her duty to punish me, because I'm a man, and all men are nothing but filthy dogs who hurt women."

I didn't know how to respond. "I'm Z."

Sniveling, he wiped his face with the back of his shaky hand. "...Peter."

"I used to be a prostitute, and the johns weren't very nice. I never thought anyone would treat me better than trash...but one man did. I know he's looking for me." I stood next to the bed and held out my hand. "Maybe if we work together, we can get out of here."

I helped him stand and get dressed. I'd discovered men's clothes, clean and folded, in a dresser drawer. He'd been lying on his back for so long that his legs were weak. We exited the room, his arm slung around my neck like I was a crutch. But we were forced to stop short because the psycho bitch from hell was standing in the hallway.

"We wouldn't leave!" he strained in a tremulous voice.

Peter struggled in vain. He was too frail and emotionally beaten to a pulp to put up a real fight. His punishment was to suffer disgrace, and mine was to witness it. She quickly subdued him. Hog-tied in the center of the bed, Peter let out cries of torment. To say Maxine was sadistic was an understatement. She was malicious—the lowest of the low. I gritted my teeth and looked in the opposite direction, wishing I could plug my ears. As much as I wanted to save Peter from the profound humiliation he was experiencing, I could do nothing.

When she'd finished assaulting him, she staggered away from the bed like a drunkard. Evidently, she'd got a rush. I glanced at the bed; Peter's bindings had been removed, and he'd tucked his knees tight to his chest and curled into the fetal position. I was thankful for one thing: Brody wasn't sadistic. That didn't exonerate him for his murders, but he seemed to have his own warped logic, and he followed it religiously. Maxine's moral compass was definitely busted.

CHAPTER SIX

*T*hat night I hardly slept a wink. Internally, I was in turmoil. I couldn't get Brody off my mind. It had been three days, and still no sign of my knight in shining armor. I began to worry. *Maybe I am expendable.*

Maxine sat on the love seat opposite me, flashing her white panties again as she crossed her legs. "Worried, huh?" She looked at me with an over exaggerated expression of woe, her lips in a swollen pout.

I rolled over to face the back of the couch and curled the blanket snug under my chin. "No."

"Liar. There was trepidation in your eyes. Well, I can tell you one thing for certain: Brody never gives up what's his."

"We don't treat each other like that," I grumbled.

"Make no mistake, little prince. He owns you." She giggled.

She'd hit the bull's-eye. He did own me, heart and soul. But she had no right to say it. Our relationship was none of her business. And it upset me so bad that I couldn't stop my mouth from running. "That sounded a bit envious."

"Pardon?"

I switched to my other side again and looked her in the eyes.

"Now I know why you kidnapped me," I said with gentle disdain. "You're *dying* for the Reaper's undivided attention. Maybe you've got some type of teacher-student fetish."

She sat back, folding her arms. "Is that supposed to piss me off?"

An idea came to me; it was just a shot in the dark, but I flashed a wry grin. "I know he makes your panties wet."

Her stern expression twitched, and she flung something metallic in my direction. I froze; a knife was sticking in the armrest. I swallowed the knot lodged in my throat and slowly sat up; I'd lost all interest in taunting her.

"What did ya think? That he liked to visit you? That you were so fucking pretty he couldn't resist slapping down hundreds a night? You and that scumbag pimp of yours were marked, dumb-ass. Marked for extermination. Because Gino got in over his head with the gangs—owed them a mountain of cash. And whenever there's gang involvement, there's more prostitution, more drugs, and more death. The government will only tolerate so much illegal activity. And when they've had enough of being undermined, End Life comes in."

For a second time, my blood ran cold, and I shivered. "You're lying again!"

"Then tell me—how did you two meet, huh? How did Brody become your client? It ain't like you move around in the same social circles, now do ya?"

I didn't have an answer. "I don't know! He just showed up one day."

"I realize you're dense, but even that kind of bullshit's gotta cause a light to flicker."

"Shut up!"

"What? Are you gonna cry now? Oh, boo hoo." She mock-pouted. "I'm not like Brody. He's special. He was born a psychotic sociopath, and he doesn't give two shits what happens to you or anyone else on this planet. I admit I'm a little crazy, but I'm a product of a bad environment. Which means, I have an legitimate excuse."

"Bullshit! You have orgasms when you kill." I glared at her, digging my nails into the armrest. "You're just in denial. You're the worst kind of person...a habitual liar."

She pounced, clearing the coffee table, and closed the gap between us in a fraction of a second before backhanding me in the face. It felt like a brick had clocked me. Hanging my head, I tried to focus on the floor as blood trickled from my nose. "Get it through your dumbass pea brain. Brody doesn't love you. Serial killers don't love. We're incapable." She lifted my wet chin and searched my watery eyes. "We destroy everything we touch. And that destruction gives us a euphoric high—gratification that's better than any drug. I'm telling you, it's better than sex. That's what makes us killers. So if you think Brody cares about you, you're delusional." She straightened and put her hand on her thin hip. "Trust me, when he no longer feels fulfilled, he will dispose of you just like all his other victims."

"You're wrong!"

"Do you think if you shout it won't make it so? The facts remain."

You're wrong! I squeezed my eyes shut and grabbed my own hair; I refused to believe that all the kind things he'd done were just hollow promises, sentiment intended to appease me. "If he wanted me dead, he would've done it in the beginning."

"I admit, I don't have clue what he's thinking when it comes to you. If it were me I would've fucked you then slit your throat." She kicked my sneakers. "Put them on."

"Why?"

She held up the knife. "This time I won't miss."

Bitch.

I tied my shoelaces, my heart once again thudding. She bound my wrists and put a blindfold over my eyes. Then she pushed me out of the apartment and into an elevator, which made my stomach lurch when it came to a bouncy stop. I couldn't see more than periodic flashes of brightness through the fabric. I heard a door shut, and cold, crisp air wafted my face and arms; I wasn't wearing a jacket. We were outside.

She kept a firm grip on my arm. And after we'd walked for a considerable distance, she tugged, and I stood still. Without any bearings, I didn't dare move a muscle.

"Well, little prince, let's see if you can attract the big ol' owl."

She booted me in the ass and I tripped forward, stretching my arms out stiffly for fear of falling. "See you soon!"

Her laughter rang in the air then grew fainter and fainter. I tore off the blindfold to find that I'd been dumped on a dark street slick with fresh snowfall. And I couldn't see my captor anywhere; she'd vanished. Shivering, I picked at the bindings and worked my wrists free. Dropping the twine, I looked nervously around. The area was deserted and bordered by derelict apartment blocks. It gave me the heebie-jeebies. I'd never done well alone in the dark.

Moving backward with a jittery bounce in my step, I turned abruptly to make a run for it. But a wraithlike figure manifested in the street. Pistol aimed, Brody walked straight toward me. I was astonished; it was like Maxine had known he'd be waiting.

"Are you all right?" he asked, lowering the gun.

"Yeah."

He searched my eyes as if he didn't believe me. "The truth?"

"She's a sadistic bitch, but she didn't touch me."

"Like a cat, she enjoys toying with her prey." The tone of his voice expressed relief; otherwise, I sensed nothing else from him. He looked past me to a partially lit building a mile up the road, and removed his ski jacket. "Which floor is her suite?"

"Sixth. It's the penthouse, I think. Oh, and, there's another guy. She keeps him locked inside the second bedroom."

He handed me the jacket. "Name?"

"Peter," I said, slipping my arms inside the welcoming warmth. I'd forgotten how cold it was—my extremities were numb. When Maxine had released me, I was thankful, but now that we were heading back into the lion's den, I began to seriously worry. "You don't have to kill her. I can call the cops."

"She will never cease pursuit, Zeus."

I knew that no matter what I said, it would come down to a fight. It was what they both wanted. Maxine needed to prove herself, and Brody needed to obliterate the evil that threatened my life.

CHAPTER SEVEN

$\mathcal{T}$he lobby smelled musty as we made our way to the emergency exit stairwell. By the time we'd reached the sixth floor, I was bent over, trying to catch my breath. Brody was the same as usual, unruffled and seemingly in his element. A solid steel door stood between the sixth floor and us.

"There's something you're not telling me," I whispered at his back.

Placing a firm grip on the knob, he eyed me. "This is the first time two professionals have gone up against one another outside a controlled environment."

"You mean this is like...a test?"

"In all probability." He drew a gun from his left holster. "I am about to meet her in a secure, private location. The invitation can't be misconstrued."

By 'invitation,' he was referring to my kidnapping. Thanks to me, the bitch had lured out my lover.

Once he opened the door, we were in a rectangular foyer with brown Berber carpeting and an elevator. The only other exit was the entrance to Maxine's large suite.

He pressed two fingers to my chest. "Wait here."

"But the place is huge, and you don't know the layout. She could be hiding anywhere."

"Precisely."

I frowned. I was well aware that Brody could handle himself, but Maxine was crazy. The door shut in my face—he'd vanished. I waited and waited. Then I felt an unnerving presence at my back.

"God, you must be one a hell of a piece of ass for the grand master to actually make an appearance."

The hairs lifted on my nape and arms. She'd snuck like a mouse into the foyer. I froze, scared to breathe, as something razor-sharp caught me just under my ribcage on my right side, through the ski jacket.

She grabbed the scruff of my neck and a fistful my hair. "How long has he been inside?"

"Less than a minute." It was an awkward position, and I almost fell over. "Come on, don't pull so hard!"

"Keep your voice down," she hissed near my ear. "We're going in. But here's the thing: Brody's unpredictable, so you're gonna stay in front of me."

"I get it, like a shield."

"No heroics, little prince." She pressed the blade deeper. "Or you will get hurt."

I did as I was told, even though it was difficult to walk a straight line with her pulling on my hair. I carefully opened the door and shuffled through a wide hallway that fanned out into a huge kitchen-dining-living area with a vaulted ceiling and massive windows on the southern wall. The soulful words of Yuya Matsushita, a singer she would constantly listen to, filled the space, lending an odd feel to the situation. That was when Brody confronted us. I felt a tad uneasy, since his gun was pointed at me. Maxine maneuvered me backward between the furniture.

"Well, well, well...if it ain't '*the Reaper*.'" Her voice rang with bitter contempt; she envied him.

"It's been a long time, Maxine."

"Come now, what's with the sad face? You know how the

game's played. The top brass aren't happy. They invested a lot of time and money. They can't have their finest asset running wild."

"Considering the natural state of my mind, they had to invest nothing. There's no need to convince a killer to do as he or she has been programmed."

"A genetic mutation, then?" she asked. "Or have you always been an arrogant asshole?"

He stepped nearer. "Verbal threats demonstrate incompetence and a lack of couth. I'm here. I don't need to be baited. Release him and you'll live."

"That's not the deal," she said. "You're going to return with me to End Life. After that you will kiss Doctor Günter's ass and make amends for all the trouble you've caused. And then I might release him."

Brody wasn't impressed or moved by her speech, although his indifferent expression suggested that it wasn't unexpected. "You know I won't dignify that with an answer."

"Oh, well, such is life." She yanked my head back, and something punctured my flesh just below my ribcage. The knife went in to the hilt before she pulled it out. Pain shocked my system to the core, and I clutched my side. I looked down; blood was running between my violently shaking fingers like water over rocks. And it dripped on the circular area rug, tiny rubies on creamy velvet. I went down for the count.

Brody's gaze hardened to ice, and he pressed the trigger. The semi-automatic discharged shells into the air. Maxine ducked and ran as bullets tore holes in the drywall and shattered everything they came in contact with. Objects exploded. Debris flew. And I tried desperately to find something to stuff into the oozing hole in my side. If I'd learned anything from reading all those books the two years while Brody went rogue, it was that I had to stop the bleeding. I pawed at a table runner draping the coffee table, and everything fell onto the area carpet.

She sprang forward and swiped with both blades, slicing Brody's forearm and chest. He jumped back, red soaking through his gray shirt. He briefly examined his blazer sleeve. Then she rushed him, chopping with her arm. He discarded the gun and blocked the strike, and a second, as she tried to drive the blades into his face. She struck repeatedly, like lightning—here, there, and everywhere—and he swiftly shifted from side to side to avoid each jab. The sequence of their fighting was like a martial arts movie.

Amazingly, Brody never wavered. He remained focused as he always did. Hitting her arm, he knocked the knife from her grasp. When she lost her footing, he gripped her blazer and bashed her into the shelving unit. The disc player shifted, and the music skipped. The sound of scraping crackled through the speakers, and Yuya Matsushita belted out 'She's a Liar.' The rhythm and blues piece added a comical ambience to their battle.

She kneed him in the torso, broke free, did a back flip, and kicked him in the chops. He fell into a wall, his arms spread.

Beat up as Brody was, he continued to fight. There seemed to be no stopping him. He was like a machine that fed off her brutality and made it his own. He rose from between toppled furniture and punched her in the gut, chest, and jaw, and she stumbled backward into the adjoining hallway. Dazed, she still swung, but her efforts appeared slightly off the mark.

"Why him?"

"He's mine."

"We don't love," she snarled. "We're incapable!"

"I disagree."

"Love is a meaningless emotion!"

"Meaningless to some, consequential to others." His gaze was on fire as he breathed in her face. "My reasons are beyond your psychological capacity."

He decked her over and over, slowly breaking her, and the stress seeped from her pores; her sweaty complexion exuded terror. She tried to slash him, but he twisted the second knife from her grasp, and I swear I heard a bone snap; it sounded just like a brittle twig. She wailed and belted his mouth.

Feeling weary, as if I hadn't slept in days, I settled in completely, wedged between the coffee table and couch.

They came in and out of focus.

Brody dropped to a crouch, stabbed her quick in the diaphragm, spun around in the same hunched position, and stung her twice again, like a scorpion. Stunned, she clutched at the wounds and staggered in the direction of the main entryway.

Rising to stand, he cocked his head with a crack and glided into the abyss after her, his knife dripping and a glint of death in his razor-sharp smile. The mouthy bitch in thigh-high leather didn't have a hope in hell. Not that I had any sympathy. I didn't, since we were both meeting our end.

There was another, briefer, scuffle before she walked unsteadily into the living room, tripping over the area carpet with blood trailing her steps. He followed, calm as always. Then he got in her face, grabbed her by the throat, and squeezed. She struggled, frenzied, her limbs flailing, and he rushed a few steps forward and slammed her into a wall. She gouged the soft pockets of flesh around his eyes. But he lifted her until only the toes of her boots touched the floor. His steely-gray gaze turned silver, and he clenched his jaw, his arms vibrating.

I'd never seen the kind of strength that could lift another person off the floor. But then, his strength was fueled by bloodlust. When Brody lost it, he became another man, a darker persona— the shell of a human I hardly recognized.

Maxine convulsed and sloppily cuffed his face in a last-ditch effort to inflict pain. But eventually her aggression lessened. Then her arms fell limp and a hollow sounding expulsion of air escaped her parted lips, lips that had turned bloated and blue. Eyes watery and lifeless, she stared at him. After a moment of thoughtful assessment, he kissed her on the mouth with tenderness. Grimaced. Pinned her skull to the wall. And slit her throat.

She dropped to the floor with a weighty thud.

The CD player skipped, and 'She's a Liar' filled the quiet space once again.

Brody stepped over her and came toward me, debris crunching under the soles of his boots. He knelt, took hold of my arm, grabbed the waist of my jeans, and lifted. Slung over his shoulder like a sack of potatoes, I traveled down six flights of steps and out onto the street. The last thing I remembered was pavement and buildings passing my blurring line of sight.

~

I AWOKE IN A HOTEL ROOM, in a queen-size bed, with an intravenous drip in my arm. Candles lit the room. And the faint scent of Brody's cologne hung in the air. I tried to move, but the shooting pain in my abdomen wouldn't let me. I turned my head and saw him seated at the small table cleaning his Berettas. He was meticulous as always.

Without acknowledging me, he asked, "How do you feel?"

I gingerly touched my bandaged waist. "Better."

"Good." He shoved a magazine into the gun. "I cleaned the wound before stitching it. No vital organs were pierced. I also administered a shot of antibiotics and a strong painkiller. You have to remain stationary for a least a week to recover properly. Too much movement may split the stitches and rupture the newly healing tissue."

"You sure know a lot about everything."

He grinned, polishing the muzzle. "I absorb everything I hear, see, taste, touch, and feel. I am what you'd call hypersensitive with an overactive brain."

"Does it bother you?"

"No. I've learned to control the intake."

"I've always wanted to ask... What's your IQ?"

"Every test for End Life produced a different score, which is normal, as question content varies. I consecutively scored between 159 and 170."

I didn't know a lot, but I figured that anyone with brains over 140 was extremely intelligent. All of a sudden, I felt quite inferior.

No matter how much knowledge I acquired, I'd never measure up to Brody. I quickly changed the subject.

"What about Peter?"

"He's in a hospital."

"You did help him...."

He glanced at me. "I caught the hint of surprise in your voice. I may be a killer, but I'm not a savage."

I chuckled then clutched my side, groaning; it hurt like hell to laugh. "That's kind of a contradiction in terms. ...I feel sort of stoned, but good. Those painkillers must be working great."

He quietly sniggered, and I gawked at him. I'd never heard him laugh before. I never knew he was capable of displaying real happiness.

"You're even more handsome when you're happy."

"Don't tease."

"I'm serious. Hell, I got a raging boner just thinking about it."

Brody set the gun and cloth on the table and put his hands on his legs. "Any rigorous activity will more than likely split the stitches."

"Anal isn't the only way to have sex."

Next thing I knew, the chair was pushed away from the table and he was pulling his shirt up over his head. "Don't worry, I'll be gentle," he said.

"Who's worried?"

There'd been excitement in his voice—another first. My hopes rose a little higher. *Maybe he does love me.*

I got comfortable beside him; the sex was pretty awesome, but I had something else on my mind. "Was I marked before? Is that why you became my client?"

He was silent for a period then sighed with an air of regret. "Yes. Indirectly. The government determined the Regent and whoever was running it had to be exterminated," he explained. "As with any complex job, I always map out the surroundings and take an inventory of the intended targets. The Regent was like Sodom and Gomorrah. Abraham bargained with God that if ten faithful souls were found he'd spare the cities. I decided if I found one good soul I'd spare the hotel. And I found you."

Flopping a bent arm over my face, I fought back the anxiety. I couldn't help but get upset; it was like water rising in a well, threatening to overflow.

He hugged me and kissed the back of my arm. "I entered the lobby and you were with an intoxicated man. You seemed out of place in the filth around you...confused in a world out of your control. I knew you didn't belong there. You were beautiful, a beauty among beasts. I had to have you."

He eased his mouth closer and we kissed. I sniffed, searching his eyes as he wiped the burn of tears from my cheeks, his thumbs smoothing my flesh.

"I'm not beautiful."

"You are. You're perfection itself."

I didn't understand the fascination, but for whatever reason, he seemed to genuinely care about me. Against the wishes of End Life, he'd saved me. A serial killer had taken me in and cherished me like one of his mother's fine porcelain dolls.

Maybe that's how he saw me.

I was a doll.

THE NEXT MORNING when we were leaving, the front desk gave Brody a message written on a plain slip of beige paper.

Thanks to a fresh snowfall during the night, the city lay dormant, the scenery changed to that of sleepy English winter wonderland like something out of a Jane Eyre novel. We stood in the city square, snow swirling past our boots, as one of the payphones continued to ring and ring, an endless disruption to the tranquility. Brody entered the booth and put the receiver to his ear. I snuggled against him and he allowed me to listen in. The line clicked.

Brody didn't use a formal greeting. Instead, he said in a monotone, "She's in the penthouse suite on Garvis."

"We know," a man with a German accent replied.

"Then we have nothing further to discuss."

"You beat and stabbed her, choked her to death then slit her throat. Quite brutal."

"A moderately befitting end for the queen of sadism."

"You won't get away with this, Brody. We know how you think. We also know about your whore—the man you protect. He's weak and will slow you down."

"Whore is erroneous and past tense."

"The government is involved. If you come home right now, I may still be able to convince them to not press charges. Everything you've done could be swept under the carpet."

"I will let Providence decide." He placed the receiver on the hook.

The moment he hung up on that man, I knew our lives would be thrust into turmoil once again. Maxine certainly wouldn't be the last assassin to come after us. Brody had told me that aside from one other professional End Life had a secret list of apprentice killers at their disposal, people they could put through the Snuff program. But, to date, he was the only one to successfully complete all the rigorous physiological tests and physical exams. Which meant that the pharmaceutical giant would never allow him—their best asset— to quit. Brody knew too much. He'd become a liability and a threat. Especially since he knew the inner workings of the company.

He walked ahead through the blowing snow, and I rushed to catch up. I don't know why, but I tried to bolster his confidence. Perhaps if I maintained some type of optimism, he would too.

"I have faith in you," I said.

"This isn't a game, Zeus."

"I realize that, but I still want you to know...I trust you, and I love you."

He stopped and, without looking, held out a gloved hand. The faintly affectionate gesture sent my pulse racing. Maybe my words were slowly sinking in. I slid my hand in his, and our fingers locked.

"You still love me," he said with quelled delight.

Yeah, like crazy. If I didn't touch him at least once a day, I'd die. Cease to be. I didn't know adequate words to describe the never-ending storm that raged inside me, that swung between wanting him and not wanting him. But if I kept things simple, perhaps eventually my feelings would get through to him.

"More than anything," I replied, and his mouth curled into a mischievous grin.

JACK THE ANTHROPOPHAGITE

Book Three

AUTHOR'S NOTE

If you've come this far, then you're about to read the third install-ment in my Reaper series, *Jack the Anthropophagite*. I dare you to say that fast three times. If you can't, don't worry; I can scarcely pronounce it properly myself. Strange as it might sound, I wanted a title that would stand out and, perhaps, make potential readers pause for thought.

Brody's next opponent is Jack. Less agile than Maxine, but far more cunning, he's another serial killer with a grisly past. Jack is the oldest of the End Life inductees. At over fifty, he has accumu-lated more kills than Brody and Maxine combined. What is an anthropophagite? Well, you'll just have to read the story to find out.

Jack Sprat

Jack will eat not fat, and Jull doth love no leane.
Yet betwixt them both they lick the dishes cleane.

– From the English proverb in John Clarke's collection of sayings (1693)

CHAPTER ONE

Spring—a beautiful, green-eyed maiden, her sable hair flowing and bare flesh sprinkled with flowers in a rainbow of colors—rode the horizon, tempting old man Winter to follow her. Prying the world from his icy clutches, she brought temperate rain to melt the snow and warm his heart. Bit by bit the frost bitten meadow turned verdant, and the gray skies were blue once again. Sunshine cut a rift between the clouds and illuminated the dewy grass. And everything that had been dead was reborn.

I touched the condensation on the kitchen window, and a droplet trickled to the bottom of the pane. The aromatic scent of meatballs simmering in a pot filled with crushed tomatoes, basil, and oregano made my stomach grumble. Brody should've been a chef. And I thoroughly enjoyed eating whatever he was willing to serve. As a consequence, I overindulged and had gained eighteen pounds in just a few months. I didn't care for the added weight, but Brody said that I looked healthier. His way of complimenting me, I'm sure.

Before, I was skinnier, a reflection of the bad situation we were in at that time. Whenever my anxiety took hold and I stressed out, weigh loss was a given side effect. Pharmaceutical giant End Life had sent one of their assassins, Maxine, the sadistic bitch from hell, to kill Brody and me. During the ordeal she'd taken me hostage, something I tried hard to forget. Even though she could never harm me again, I still languished with nightmares. Brody believed the attack was a warning, and there was more yet to come. So after Maxine's death, we'd stayed at various motels throughout the prairies until I'd crossed paths with a charitable farmer from the town of Meadowhill.

Mr. McMurty owned acres of agricultural land, primarily wheat, but a few were dedicated to sunflowers and corn. And at the west end of his property stood a farmstead in a state of disrepair: the original structure his great-grandfather had built. He offered us lodgings in the century-old house and in exchange I did odd jobs while Brody worked to fix the place. Once again we were back to living with only the basics. The yard had a small fenced vegetable garden, a chicken coop, and a few ancient fruit trees that had withered into knotted branches and gnarled roots. The house had several bedrooms, a kitchen, a larder and storeroom, a parlor, and a set of creaky wood steps that led to a loft blanketed in spider webs. The furniture probably predated the house. But thankfully the place had indoor plumbing—a welcome upgrade from the cottage in Beisicker.

Other than Mr. McMurty, we relied on local gossip and a transistor radio to provide news from the outside world. More often than not, the gossip turned out to be more accurate.

Brody placed a steaming bowl of pasta in front of me—a swirly mountain of spaghetti noodles topped with half a dozen golf-ball-sized meatballs. Mashing my cigarette in the ashtray, my stomach grumbled in anticipation. The food smelled delicious.

But just as I was about to stick my fork in, the front door rattled with a knock. We both looked in the direction of the parlor. Brody rose from the table and I followed at an unwilling pace, my gaze transfixed on the food. *Damn, I'm starving.*

Brody opened the door to a gust of damp wind that swirled around my ankles and Mr. McMurty on the porch, wearing mud-caked work boots and stained coveralls that were two sizes too big. His wisp of white hair stood on end, his dark eyes sparkled, and the wrinkles around his mouth were etched into a permanent smile. He was a kindly, little old man, and one of the nicest people I'd ever met—Santa Claus in the flesh.

"Sorry to bother ya, lads."

"Would you like to come in?" asked Brody.

"If you don't mind for a minute." He smiled warmly and removed his boots. "I hope it isn't too much trouble, but the rain does something awful to my bones this time of year."

"No trouble," Brody said.

Yes, it is an inconvenience...for my stomach, I bitched inside my head. My lover's friendly neighbor routine grated on my nerves. He knew how irritable I got when I was hungry. I exhaled an annoyed sounding sigh, and he smirked at me.

"I was wondering if you're busy this afternoon. My tractor is giving me fits again." He tottered into the parlor, but stopped to sniff at the air like a bloodhound. "Oh my, it smells good in here."

"That's our lunch," I said.

"Lunch... Then I have interrupted."

"Think nothing of it." Brody gestured to the kitchen like a butler. "Would you care to join us?"

I stared at him in amazement; he'd never shown an amiable attitude toward anyone other than me. Then again, Mr. McMurty was harmless and wifeless, which meant he was lonely.

"Well, I..."

"Sure, come on." I touched his shoulder, a bony ledge under his clothes. "Before it gets cold."

He looked at us both. "I appreciate the offer, lads, but I've got a pot of chicken soup on the stove. It's the tractor I'm worried about."

"What's the problem?"

"I think it may have a blockage in the fuel line or filter. Halfway to town it started sputterin' and wheezin', then it died. I can't see as good as I used to, that's why I was hoping you could lend me a hand again."

"Of course," Brody assured him.

"Thanks. Well, I best get back to the house."

After reheating our food, Brody sat across from me. I shoveled a heaping forkful into my mouth; the tangy richness of garden fresh vegetables and spices hit my taste buds. "Mmm... This is good," I remarked. "The sauce is really thick."

"As it should be."

"True. But these meatballs are the best." I cut the largest one in half with my fork.

"Evidently, my culinary skills are satisfactory." He grinned. "After we're done, I'll help Mr. McMurty."

Wiping the corners of my mouth with a napkin, I chuckled. "And what do you know about farm equipment mechanics?"

"Nothing. But I must abide by our arrangement."

We continued to eat, but in silence.

The deal we'd made with Mr. McMurty bothered me. I savored the last morsel and pushed my chair away from the table, picking up my bowl and cutlery. "I don't think we should stay here any longer."

"You're concerned."

Cranking the taps, I squirted dish soap into the rolling water. "Well, I think I have a right to be, after everything that's happened. This is the longest we've stayed in one place. I don't want to get too comfortable. We attract trouble, and Mr. McMurty doesn't deserve that."

Brody put his dishes in the kitchen sink and surprised me with a kiss. "We'll discuss it later."

With my forearms sunk in suds, I watched him put on his jacket and exit through the front entry of the house. The screen door creaked after the interior one shut. "Good luck," I said to a quiet room. Even minutes after his departure, I could still feel the burn of his breath on my lips. He didn't kiss me often. It seemed like he had to remind himself that it was normal behavior between a pair of romantically involved people.

I dried the dishes and hung the tea towel over the counter; there were chores to finish.

~

BY FOUR THIRTY, I packed it in. Mopping sweat from my brow, I cast my gaze skyward to see dark clouds moving in. I hung the gardening tools inside the shed, leaned the wheelbarrow against the interior wall, and backed out to shut and padlock the doors. The rain came down hard like sticks on a snare drum, striking the shed with a barrage of metallic pings, and my boots sank in the quagmire before I dashed for the house. Breathing deeply, I slammed the screen door; I'd left a trail of muddy prints on the porch. I set my boots on a tray next to the entrance and walked through the hallway and into the bathroom, tugging my shirt and wool sweater over my head.

The shower didn't get as hot as I wanted, but it still soothed my aching bones. Stepping onto the braided, slate blue bathmat, I grabbed a towel. Brody had been gone all day, and I wondered how he'd made out with the repairs. He'd studied several books at the local library, a building no bigger than a construction site portable.

I wiped away the layer of moisture on the window to see a tall scarecrow of a man with grubby overalls and gaunt cheeks staring at me from the yard, his long, scraggly hair blowing in the windy rain. I immediately ducked and slowly wiped my mouth with the towel. *Who the hell is that*? For a split second my brain went haywire. I couldn't remember if I'd locked the front door or if the rest of the windows throughout the house were shut.

Where did I put the pistol?

Think, think, think...

I was alone, naked, and vulnerable. Crouching, I scrambled out of the bathroom and darted through the hall, shutting off the light as I went. I snuck into the dark bedroom and threw on my clothes, all the while glancing back at the window. Brody and Mr. McMurty would return at any moment. I hoped.

In the kitchen, I removed the lid on the cookie jar, a beige ceramic jug with cracked glaze, and reached inside. The gun had a rough grip, and I wrapped my fingers around it. Lightning struck as I stood to the side of the front window, opened the drape by a fraction of an inch, and peered outside. But there was no one. I snuck from room to room, locking all the windows and shutting the curtains. But I never saw anyone. Eventually, I slumped into a chair and shakily set the pistol on the kitchen table. Then I stared into the gloom, listening to the howling wind and rain. I didn't turn on the lights because I feared that whoever was outside might see me.

One hour.

Two hours.

Nearly three hours passed before I heard someone on the front porch fiddling with the deadbolt. I snatched the gun, padded softly to the front of the house, and turned on a lamp. With a gust of chilly wind, Brody appeared inside the parlor. He shut the door and stared at me—lenses frosted with moisture, hair stringy like a mop head, and clothes soaked through.

"I assume it's loaded this time," he said calmly.

I'd forgotten about the pistol, and looked at it for a moment in bewilderment. "Ah, yeah, it's loaded. Sorry if I startled you."

Unfazed as usual, his expression was indifferent. "Evidently, there's a reason why you're holding a loaded gun in the dark."

"About that..." I frowned, squeezing the grip. "After I got out of the shower, I saw a man in the yard. I freaked and closed all the curtains and turned off the lights."

He held out his hand and I passed the gun to him. "Lock the door behind me. I'll be back shortly."

~

THE HOUSE FELT DAMP, so I started a fire, waiting and warming my hands in silence. Soon as the screen door creaked, I sprang to my feet, anxious for news. "Well?"

Brody pushed back his wet hood and unzipped his jacket. "I found nothing. Not a trace of human activity."

"It figures. His footprints are probably under several inches of rainwater by now."

Lightning illuminated the sparsely furnished parlor—dull fabrics and wooden objects loosely connected by elongated shadows. The room was small, maybe twelve by fourteen, and the drapes were heavy and faded from the sun. I didn't like the idea of that man peering in through any of the windows, so I had untied the drapes and drawn them together. Brody locked both the screen and front doors. The old deadbolt and chain were easy to break, but if someone did try it, they would make noise.

Brody padded past and I followed so close I almost tripped him. "Do you plan to join me?"

"Huh?" I gawked at him, momentarily confused.

He gripped the bathroom doorknob, crystal set in a tarnished brass fitting. "Normally, I wouldn't mind, but tonight I'm exhausted."

"Oh!" I snorted with nervous laughter and put up my hands. "Sorry, I didn't mean to— I'll leave you alone."

He knew exactly why I had followed, whimpering like a scolded dog, and he drew me into a hug. I immediately put my head on his chest and held him tight. His grimy T-shirt smelled of engine grease, his body radiated clammy warmth, and I could hear the slow and soothing rhythm of his heart.

I wanted to stay in that position forever; his strong embrace provided emotional contentment as well as a sense of physical security, something I'd never experienced growing up in the whorehouse. Prostitutes didn't make for outstanding parents. Most were too strung out to give a shit, and saw me as little more than a nuisance. The only thing that saved my ass was my introverted, cowardly nature and the fact I ran errands. I spent more time purchasing prophylactics and the morning-after pill than anything else.

For whatever reason, Brody was able to interpret my mood, because he always gave me hug when I needed it the most.

"I'd like to shower, Zeus."

"Oh, sure!" I released him and weakly smiled. "Sorry."

He kissed my forehead before disappearing inside the bathroom. Stunned, I touched the spot where he'd kissed me. The tender gesture lingered, the heat blossoming on my skin.

Why did you kiss me again?

CHAPTER TWO

An additional search of the property the next morning yielded nothing. All the outbuildings appeared undisturbed. The storm had turned the yard into a mud bath that would take at least a week for the ground to absorb. So no footprints, not even vehicle tracks, were found from the night before.

I stood near the shed with my hands in my jacket pockets and peered over my shoulder. A blast of wind blew Brody's hair forwards. "I guess I've got an overactive brain. Sorry."

"I've said it countless times, Zeus: never apologize."

"But I feel stupid. It's like the guy was a figment of my imagination or something." Disappointed with myself, I sighed and turned in the direction of the house. "We haven't eaten yet and I'm starved. What do you want for breakfast?"

"You." He didn't grin, but his eyes sparkled.

The anticipation fluttered through my chest, my cock began to swell, and my thoughts scattered. I was too excited to think straight, and my arms fell limp at my sides. *Sex. Now.* He lightly brushed my neck with his rough fingers and I shivered, laughing. Then I let out a muffled groan as he pressed his mouth to mine, embracing me hard. His hot breath seared my skin as he covered my chin and throat with fervent kisses.

The more time we spent together, the more Brody's serial killer persona seemed to disappear. I don't know if he'd skewed my sense of humanity or logic, or a combination of both, but he'd simply become my lover.

Shutting the front door, he removed his boots as I backed into the parlor. "Strip," he said evenly.

"What...? Here? Now?"

"Yes. Yes. And yes."

"What if Mr. McMurty sees us?" I motioned to the large front window that captured an unobstructed view of nearly a third of the farm, then gulped as he yanked the drapes shut. "I guess that solves that problem."

"Anything else?"

"N-no, I don't th-think so."

"The odd instance when you stammer gives me a rush."

"Really." I bumped into the couch as he pulled his T-shirt over his head and dropped it on the floor.

Next thing I knew he had me bent over the couch in my favorite position. With the natural downward curve of his erection, I felt more when we did it doggie. He spread my ass and his tongue dug into my opening, rushing sparks of excitement straight to my belly. I gripped the cushions, pulse rising with the slick insertion of his lubed fingers. He slowly worked them in and out while massaging my stiff length. Then I exhaled tensely as the engorged head of his cock slid past my rim and in deep. But the mild discomfort soon vanished as he began to pump. I moaned over and over, holding on. My cock kept nudging the plush velvet back of the couch as he drove me from behind. He felt good, hot and hard, repeatedly filling me to the hilt. In minutes, I was on the verge of total ecstasy.

I grabbed myself, but then his breath was on my shoulder, and I hesitated.

"Don't masturbate. Let yourself go," he whispered with a searing heat, and my skin tingled.

His words got my heart pounding faster; I'd never had a prostate-assisted orgasm. He eased out, leaving me cold and empty. But then I gasped, quickly arching my spine as he again inserted his fingers, coated in more lube, and began to stimulate my prostate. The flutter of movement in the right spot and... I suddenly cried out as an orgasm tore through my groin and warmed my face. I didn't realize until after I'd fainted that he'd stroked my cock and I'd ejaculated in conjunction with a second orgasm.

"Did you enjoy it?"

I frowned and shakily rose from the couch; my legs had turned to jelly. "Yeah, it felt awesome, but what about you?"

"Your pleasure is my pleasure." He put on his shirt and tucked the hem inside his jeans.

"That's not fair...to you."

He zipped his fly. "The local diner serves breakfast until noon."

"But..." I stared at him for a moment, wondering why I'd received special treatment. When he held out my jacket, I knew there would be no explanation. He had his reasons. "Right. Give me a minute." I shut the bathroom door and used a warm, soapy facecloth to clean myself. Then I dressed. The sex was great, but surprisingly one-sided. Normally, he was more intense—seeking to self-gratify first. I didn't know how to handle this new and strangely sensitive Brody.

BRODY FLICKED a newspaper open as I poured cream into my coffee and stirred. Holding the mug with both hands, I scanned the diner, taking a slurp. The place was dingy, with one row of booths lining the rear wall and a horseshoe of two-person tables. The booths were upholstered in brown vinyl cracked with age. The framed, enlarged photos were faded images of a bygone era: horses pulling plows and men on tractors. We were smack dab in the country's heartland and seemingly far from our element. Our clothes weren't flashy, but we stood out—Brody with his professor-wannabe glasses and casual long-sleeved shirt, and me in my ripped jeans, heavy metal T-shirt, navy scarf, and bomber jacket. Our hair had got long. So long that his bang hung below his cheek, and mine was a kinky mess. We looked like a right pair of vagrants.

Other than an elderly couple in a booth eating breakfast, we were the only people in the joint. Holding a piece of toast, the old man passed a friendly smile, a morning greeting, and I gave a nod in response.

"Despite the fact he's lost significant weight, is this the man?" Brody asked.

I licked my fingers and took the newspaper from him. The grainy black and white image was that of a willowy man with frazzled light hair, dark beady eyes, and protruding cheekbones with tight folds of wrinkles beneath. He wasn't an amiable-looking person. He was grotesque, a ghostly spindle of a creature scarcely human in appearance. "Yeah, that's the guy," I said with genuine surprise, skimming the headline. The article stated the man, weighing a lean hundred and seventy pounds, had recently escaped a psychiatric hospital in the city. "So the guy I saw was real. Who is he?"

"Jack."

The waitress set a plate of scrambled eggs, farmer's sausage, and hash browns in front of me; Brody had an omelet and several slices of rye.

"You know of him?"

"No. I *know* him." Brody slathered peanut butter an inch thick on his toast.

During our stay in the abandoned prairie town of Beisicker, I'd discovered that Brody had a fondness for peanut butter. Kind of similar to my pimp Gino, who had loved to put ketchup on everything. Mashed potatoes, burgers, steak and eggs, you name it: no meal was safe. And Brody did the same thing. But I drew the line when it came to sex—I'd dip my dick in honey, even jam, but not peanut butter.

"Pardon?" I asked.

"Read the entire article."

Once I had reached the bottom of the last column, I'd lost my appetite. The article mentioned that Jack had been arrested twenty years ago and found guilty of a triple homicide in a small town near Beisicker. The judge ordered that he be placed in a mental institution. But instead, End Life acquired him as part of a scientific study group. As a consequence he spent more than half his sentence with the pharmaceutical corporation. I shivered at the thought. "So this means they trained Jack just like they trained you?"

"Unfortunately."

"Well, if that's the case, then we both know this 'scientific study group' is a load of bullshit." I smacked the newspaper with the back of my fingers. "It was probably the Snuff program."

He swallowed then grinned. "Excellent deduction."

Glancing around, I lowered my bitterness to a dull roar. "It was the *only* deduction. But I thought you were the first inductee."

"Jack takes that honor."

"So he's a lot older than you?"

"Significantly."

"Which means he's chalked up more kills, right?"

"If we adhere to serial killer profiling then, technically, yes. Most killers begin their quest in their mid to late teens: animals first, until they can hone their skills and, for some, develop the nerve. There are two scientific theories: first, that certain people are born killers; and second, that they are conditioned to become killers due to extreme psychological trauma—usually some type of maltreatment that happens during childhood, like repeated sexual abuse. I don't have exact figures. But I can tell you Jack is fifty-four years of age. It's simple mathematics."

I sighed, resting my head on my fist. "Wow, he's killed a shit-load of people."

"How eloquent. Perhaps an actual education would help."

I stuck out my tongue then shoved the last piece of sausage in my mouth.

Brody flashed that razor-sharp smile, pushing his glasses up his nose. "Profanity debases your intelligence."

"Yeah, but sometimes it just sounds better—you know, like saying, 'Hey, you stupid fucker! Get the fuck out of here!' Don't you ever get the urge to swear like that when you're angry?"

"No."

"You do sometimes when we have sex."

"That's different, Zeus. Every word should be used in its appropriate context."

My God, he is a robot. I kept my laughter internal. "Well, maybe you should try it some time. You might find it refreshing."

"You mean liberating."

"Same shit, just a different pile," I chuckled. I figured that if I didn't say anything, he'd never change. Then again, considering Brody's thought process, it was probably wishful thinking on my part. Maybe Maxine was right: a killer isn't capable of deep emotional attachment or basic human understanding. I finished my coffee. "Since we've figured out who my Peeping Tom is, I think we should leave town."

Brody rose from the booth, digging in his hip pocket. "I'll pay for the meal. Find a bus schedule."

In the entranceway of the restaurant was a lopsided, gold-tone metal rack filled with brochures. Most were discolored and out of date, but I did find a bus schedule. Stuffing it inside my jacket, I pushed on the exit. Outside, dark clouds blocked the sky; the weather was taking a turn for the worse. I lit a cigarette and waited on the curb adjacent to the gravel parking lot.

I glimpsed Brody as he stood beside me, zipping his jacket. "How much was the bill?"

"A pittance."

"Where to now?" Flicking ash into the wind, I stuck the cigarette in my mouth, and turned in the opposite direction, taking out the schedule.

"We need money and tickets."

e trudged the steps up to the front veranda, and Brody paused, his gaze drawn north. I automatically looked in the same direction; the main farmhouse was a field away in the distance, a glass and wood blight on the horizon. The house seemed too quiet. Then I noticed Mr. McMurty's faded two-tone Chevy pickup, still parked near the cherry tree.

My blood ran cold as ice.

"Brody, the truck..."

"It hasn't moved since yesterday." He immediately reached inside his jacket, pulled out a gun, and descended the steps to the lawn.

If Mr. McMurty wasn't sitting in his rocker reading the newspaper, we were in serious danger. Paranoid, I followed closely behind. Droplets of rain spattered Brody's shoulders and darkened sections of his hair. I looked skyward and blinked as my face was pelted. I knew it would be a downpour at any moment, and my prediction was bang on. Within a split second we were caught in a flood, and the by the time we got to the house, my runners were squelching.

The kitchen was located on the west side of the house with an entrance to the outside. We got close and heard the faint twang of country music. Brody removed his glasses, tucked them in his pocket, and carefully turned the knob. The door glided open, hinges creaking. My nostrils flared with a nauseating stench. The radio on the counter was tuned in to a local station, and there was plate of half-eaten bacon and eggs on the table. Directly ahead of us was an open archway; Brody passed through it to the next room and stopped.

Soon as I saw what he did, I fell back into the wall gasping. Mr. McMurty lay on the dining room table, clearly dead, and both his legs had been amputated mid-thigh. There was blood everywhere. My chest tightened. I clutched it and hung my head as a strange burning sensation—unnerving and upsetting—crept up the base of my skull, eating into my brain. I felt disoriented and unstable, like my whole body was about to fall apart. Then I yelped.

Brody had a gentle grip on my shoulder. "Take a deep breath."

I nodded and sucked in as much oxygen through my nose as I could, but I was soon overcome by lightheadedness. Dropping to a squat, I hugged my knees. "Oh my God, he was such a nice man!"

"True."

"This whole thing is really bad—this whole thing stinks! Now innocent people are getting killed because of me!"

Brody sighed and said flatly, "That is an erroneous assumption, Zeus. I made the decision to quit End Life. I chose to be with you."

Whether the initial blame fell on him or me didn't matter; I still felt responsible. Wiping my eyes, I gradually regained my footing. Brody holstered his Beretta.

"We've only days before the locals start to question his whereabouts."

"Should we bury him?" I wanted to cover Mr. McMurty, show some respect, and I moved almost instinctively toward him before Brody clamped my wrist.

"Do not disturb a thing."

Oh, yeah, it's a crime scene, you idiot. I nodded. Thankfully, Brody was thinking for both of us, or I'd wind up in jail. My good intentions constantly led me astray.

"Jack was part of the encampment in the mountains near Beisicker. End Life discovered the cannibals, and with the offer of fresh meat, he willingly joined the Snuff program for a part of his sentence."

I swallowed a knot. "Y-You can't be serious," I whispered. "They offered him human flesh so he'd enter their training program?"

"I thought you should be aware."

Holy fucking shit. That's why his legs are gone! I looked back at the kitchen, wondering if that was really bacon on the plate. After gagging, I asked, "Did he send...those guys...into Beisicker to kill me?"

"Although I can't prove it, I suspect End Life initiated the attack via Jack."

"Wonderful. Now I feel *so* much better."

Brody studied my expression. "I can lie if you prefer."

"You know why I'm upset, and lying isn't going to make a difference!" I fisted his damp jacket sleeve. "Please." I gave it an urgent tug. "Can we get out of here before I puke?"

CHAPTER FOUR

*E*ven though the weather was still lousy, the air outside had never smelled better. I sucked it in deeply, trying to erase the malodorous memory of decaying flesh. I couldn't even begin to imagine what a corpse would smell like after a couple of summer days locked inside. Hand on my stomach, I staggered through the rain toward the pickup, then doubled over and retched. Staring at the rocky soil, my vision blurred. I couldn't stop crying, even though I did it in silence. I squeezed my eyes shut; I don't know why, but I didn't want Brody to see. But he always knew.

He touched my lower back. "Once you feel better, we must leave."

"Yeah," I said against my fist.

We returned to the farmstead, showered and put on clean clothes, and packed our duffel bag. It was still raining when we left, and the daylight had sunk into a murky haze. Brody exited the house first, and I don't know why, but again a real uneasy feeling filled me. As I reached back to pull the door shut, a loud bang echoed off the house and blood exploded from Brody's left shoulder. The subsequent chain of frightening events happened in slow motion: the impact twisting his torso unnaturally, blood flying past his fingertips.

I couldn't expel any noise from my throat, and I couldn't move.

For a fraction of a second, time froze.

Then everything began to move at normal speed once more; Brody grabbed his shoulder, ducking for cover, and hollered, "Run!"

I instantly sprang to life, my heart pounding. I dropped the duffel bag and jumped over the veranda rail to land on the uneven ground below. And that's when I saw Jack standing in the meadow in front of the McMurty house. Rifle aimed, the pasty scarecrow fired another shot. I cringed, covering my head. Brody dove for the veranda and counter-fired with one of his M9s.

I couldn't go back inside the house. I had to get to the truck like we'd planned. The main highway ran through the town ten miles away, and it was our only means of escape. Thirty yards dead ahead, nestled on a slope, was the barn—a creosote-stained wood structure commonplace on the prairies.

Soon as I heard Brody shout "Don't stop!" I sprinted in that direction past the shed, fruit trees, and chicken coop. The daylight was almost gone as I came to a halt at the side of the barn. The gunfire had ceased. The only noise was that of the falling rain. Panting white into the air, I peered around the edge of the building. Cold droplets fell into my eyelashes and slid down my nose. I began to shiver.

Mr. McMurty's truck was an additional thousand yards away—a dangerous distance where I'd be left wide open to a bullet. *And where is Brody?* Staring at the blackening sky, I bumped the back of my head against the wall with clenched teeth. *Damn it, think!*

I sighed in defeat. With no other option, I had to make a run for it. All I could hope was that the encroaching night would camouflage my movements. I zipped my jacket to conceal my bright red T-shirt. But just as I went to run, someone clamped a hand over my mouth, giving me the scare of my life.

"It's me." Brody held me snugly, his breath in my ear.

Overwhelming relief instantly calmed me. I pried his fingers from my mouth and looked him in the eyes. "You were shot. Are you all right?"

"I won't deny the wound is a hindrance. However, I'll survive. Don't worry."

His left shoulder was weeping red; we had to get away from the farm.

"I can't help but worry."

"Aside from Jack, I've counted three other men on the property. But they keep changing locations, so I can't say with any accuracy where they're hiding. I need bait."

He had deadly aim—good enough that he could probably shoot them all blindfolded—but that wasn't my fear.

"What makes you think they won't kill me?"

"Jack covets what isn't his to take."

I knew exactly what he was getting at, though I wanted to deny it. "Your lover."

"Regrettably."

"Then he's no different from Maxine."

"Yes. He wants what I have."

"She tried to figure out why you're so fascinated with me." Clutching his jacket, I searched his eyes in desperation, once again hoping he'd tell me how he really felt. "Before I die...could you tell me why?"

As if he'd read my mind, he flashed that razor-sharp smile, held my nape, and kissed me with tenderness. It was a demonstrative gesture, just like the sex he'd done only to provide me with pleasure. It was his way of reassuring me that he loved me, even though he couldn't seem to verbalize it.

I stared as he placed one of his Berettas in my hand. The grip was solid on my skin, and it gave me—I hated to admit—a tangible sense of security.

"It's loaded. Remember to turn the safety off," he said in earnest.

"So what do you want me to do?"

"Draw the men inside the barn."

CHAPTER FIVE

rody vanished in the darkness, the squish of his footsteps absorbed by the sound of the rain. Scanning the gap from the barn to the old farmstead, I shoved the gun inside my jacket pocket. Then I mustered the courage and walked into the open, shouting, "Hey, I'm here!" At the midway point, I paused to look around again. "I know you want me." My voiced knotted in my throat. At least one man had heard me, and he was heading straight in from the meadow.

Panicked, I turned and immediately slipped, landing face down. The mud was an oil slick. Clawing at the cold muck, I clumsily got to my feet again and half-skated toward the barn.

The place smelled of dust, and my breath clouded in the dim light. My options were limited to one, so I hid in the dark amid bales of hay. Quivering, I peered through wet strands of my hair. I'd left the door open and it swung, banging the outside wall of the building. A gunshot distorted by the downpour startled me. I sank deeper between the bales. Bits of straw poked through my soaked clothes. I started covering myself with it and yanked a bale down from the top. Soon I was concealed.

The storm fiercely beat the barn, and lightning cracked the

earth like Thor's hammer, the remnants bleeding the brightest of white across the sky. The blasts of light also illuminated three men dressed in grungy hunting camouflage in the open doorway, an eerie reminder of the attack in Beisicker; the bait had worked. It was all I could do to keep my breathing shallow as I tried to get the gun out of my heavy, wet pocket.

A big, fat man approached the mountain of hay, while the others checked the loft and a line of stalls. The fat guy didn't waste time; he lifted his rifle and shot at a bale beside my head. I sprang from hiding.

My ear rang at a deafening hum as all three men grappled me and I lost my grip on the pistol. It slid under a workbench, far from my reach. My only source of protection was gone. Adrenaline pumping, I was caught in a maelstrom of violent confusion.

The fat guy laid his rifle against a stall door, took off his cap, and proceeded to unclasp his belt. I freaked, trying to wiggle free, and the guy who held my legs let go and fell backward. I pulled with my arms; the second guy lost his balance, and I kicked him. Finally free, I clambered across the floor and grabbed an old ax propped against the wall. Getting up, I swung it behind myself and hit one of the men in the gut. He landed on his rump with a groan. I swung again. Then I noticed a scythe hanging on the wall—rusted and strung with cobwebs. I ran toward it, but tripped to a dead stop when I heard the click.

"You ain't goin' nowhere." The fat guy, sweating like a stuck pig, had me in his site.

"Shoot me, then," I yelled, jabbing wearily with the ax; it had become so heavy in my fatigued state that I could hardly lift it. The gun remained out of my reach, taunting me, and I was too scared to dive for it. Maybe death would be better. "I don't care anymore—you lousy fuckers will just keep coming and coming. Yeah, I know all about End Life—them and their fucked up Snuff program."

The other two men closed in, and one of them laughed, mocking me.

Then, God knows why, I went crazy and hollered at the top of my lungs, "So kill me, pig—kill me now!"

A floorboard creaked, and just as I turned to look, Brody was there. In a split second he raised his gun, shouting, "Move!" As I ducked for cover my attackers scrambled for their weapons, but he shot the three men dead. Covered in mud and bleeding from his side, he lowered his M9, panting. He'd suffered a second gunshot wound just above his hip. I stood in front of him, hesitating to touch his injury. But he holstered his gun and grabbed my head roughly, and I unwillingly stared at him with tears streaming my face. He was pissed.

"Brody, I'm so sorry—I was going to shoot them, I really was, but I lost the gun."

He hushed me sternly and said with a ring of irritation in his voice, "Understand this: the people who hunt us have no compulsion when it comes to murder. To them you are prey, a fix to give them a rush. If you do not learn to set aside your fears, you *will* die."

"But I can't help it...I'm lousy at everything."

"You're stronger than you think."

"All right. I get it." I strained to reach under the workbench for my pistol, the grip pressing a pebbly pattern into my fingers. "I need to have self-confidence."

"Have faith."

Brody was correct. I needed to stop fretting about my lack of abilities and concentrate on what I could do. I wasn't useless anymore. My reading, writing, and vocabulary skills were much better than they were a year ago. But that wasn't what really bothered me.

What if I actually killed someone? What then? Wouldn't I be lowering myself to Jack's level? And who was the man standing in front of me? Surely he wasn't human either. They were killers, and I'd soon join them. I'd forgotten that Brody was no different than Jack: a serial killer with a bloody past, a lengthy list of victims, and a merciless, calculating temperament. I'd been blinded by love.

Brody made me look him in the eyes. "Jack is hiding," he said quietly.

"How can you be so sure?"

"It takes one to know one."

"That's not what I meant."

"You're correct; my humor was inappropriate."

"It's okay." I couldn't seem to stop crying; I was so scared he'd die and leave me. I sniffed, wiping at the river flowing down my cheeks. "But you're badly hurt."

"Get the duffel bag and head to the truck as fast as you can."

"I won't leave you. I'll help you find him."

"As soon as we step outside, he will see us regardless, Zeus."

I cast my gaze to the floor and frowned as more tears burned my sore eyes. "He's watching, then, and he heard the gunshots."

"I'm certain he's taken position near the farmstead. From there he will have a clear view of the barn door."

"Now what?"

"I want you to walk out of here and do as I have already told you."

"Grab the duffel bag and then head to the truck."

"Precisely."

I didn't want to ask, but I felt compelled; my heart ached as the words left my mouth. "How long should I wait?"

He loaded a new magazine into his gun. "Thirty minutes."

I'D WANTED to tell him to be careful or some other sentimental crap, but I couldn't do it. It would be like putting a jinx on our situation. So we parted company in silence, his bloody, soiled image forever etched into my brain.

It had finally stopped raining. The sky was clear and the moon bright.

With the gun at my side, I walked briskly in the direction of the house. When I got to the steps, the duffel bag was gone. I crouched, shoved the gun inside my pocket, and began to frantically search the length of the veranda. *It was here!*

I didn't know where Brody or the man-eating scarecrow had got to, but I needed to find our bag. Sneaking back inside the house, I stumbled in the darkness, sneakers squishing. My clothes were half wet, half dry, and uncomfortable. I tried to straighten them and that's when I saw it. The large, gray duffel bag was on the antique couch. I paused. *That's weird...*

Gunshots.

I rushed to the parlor window. My breath and the tips of my fingers fogged the glass. Someone was lying motionless on the ground near the barn. I blinked, through tears. Nothing remained but the tinkle of chimes from the front porch, and a lingering sense of dread filling my chest. Once again, I wanted to drop into the fetal position and surrender to the evil that had poisoned my life. But I couldn't.

I quickly scooped the bag into my arms and crept through the dark toward the rear door in the kitchen. Then I heard a whoosh, and something hard smacked my face.

Stunned, I groaned. I was lying flat on my back. The ceiling and cupboards were a distorted haze. I tried to get up, but the room spun and I collapsed. Rolling my head to the side, I saw the scarecrow. *The gun!* I anxiously felt my jacket pocket but it was empty. The only weapon I'd had was missing. *God, no...* He drove the snath of a scythe into the floor with a dull thud of wood on wood. The moonlight gave him a wraithlike appearance. The curved blade had blood on it.

"Where's Brody?" I mumbled.

He held the blade at an angle so the stained tip could be seen.

My heart took off thumping. "What does that mean?"

"He's dead."

The lower half of my mouth quivered, and I started to hyperventilate—every object in the room suddenly became clearer. He grabbed me. I tried to fight him off, but he punched me into submission, and the last shot felt like concrete on my jaw. Then he stripped me of my only defense, my clothes. Blood ran from my left nostril as I murmured for help that I knew would never come. If Brody hadn't walked through the door by now, he never would. The grisly scene I'd witnessed before I'd blacked out was the truth.

Jack bound my wrists with thick, coarse rope. And with a huge sledgehammer, he drove what looked like a railroad spike through the rope and into the floor. I tugged and twisted, but the rope wouldn't loosen. Hot tears flash-burned the side of my swollen face and I gasped, trembling, as Jack pried my legs apart, exposing my groin. Then he clutched my thighs and pressed my knees up into my chest. With my lower half nearly curled in a ball and my ass in the air, I couldn't move, let alone breathe.

"My, you're nice. Ripe for the pickin'." He scraped his hot, moist tongue over my scrotum and I sniveled, flexing my legs to get away. "That smug prick thought ol' Jack didn't have it in him. But I've been killin' since before he was born."

I gawked, panic-stricken, as he hunched over me, his scraggly hair raking goose bumps across my skin.

"I can smell your blood." He ground his yellow teeth into a jagged smile then snuffled my armpit like a dog sniffing a trail of scent. His hooked nose poked every private part of my body, and I flinched, yanking my arms. He ever so slowly slid the blade of a carving knife over each of my ribs, and I felt faint. Now I could see a tablecloth hanging over the edge of the kitchen table, a salt-shaker and pepper grinder, and a large frying pan on the stove. The bastard had killed Brody then prepared the room for my arrival, baiting me with the duffel bag. My fear catapulted.

"Now you're scared and your heart is beating hard. It's called an adrenaline rush. But since you can't escape, your brain will go haywire. You're gonna have the best orgasm of your life, 'cuz that's what fear does to you."

Please, God...

I heard the rustle of fabric, and I strained to look; his jeans were past his hips and he was getting into position. His erection stank of urine as he pushed it between my buttocks. "I'm going to tenderize your ass with my big cock first, then I'm gonna cut you into stewing meat."

I didn't feel the blade initially, but I did see a blotchy shadow in the archway as I lost consciousness. Something that looked like the frayed outline of an angel, I thought.

CHAPTER SIX

*T*hree bullets tore through the cannibal's back, obliterating all other noise to an eerie stillness. He stopped moving and coughed as if momentarily stunned; blood hung in a string of saliva from his chin. With the carving knife still in his hand, he exhaled a raspy, labored sigh and slowly peered over his shoulder. His face twitched, and a solitary bead of sweat trickled to his jaw. "Fuck me, you're still alive. You're one tough son-of-a-bitch."

Holding his side, Brody frowned. "He's mine from the moment he wakes in the morning to the day he takes his dying breath!"

I'd got a taste of Brody's temper when he'd battled Maxine; he'd thoroughly savored killing the crazy bitch. But with Jack, there was raw edge of bitterness in his voice, and it was wrath more than anger that seethed from each word. The tense atmosphere told me that Jack and Brody shared an especially deep-rooted malice. What had happened between them, I couldn't even begin to guess. But I sensed it was bad.

"You're like the spoiled rich kid in the sandbox," Jack sneered, bearing his rotting teeth. "He's a dumbass punk—what the hell do you see in him?"

"Everything."

"Just kill me already, you overly analytical, psychotic prick!"

Jack smirked as a fourth bullet drilled through his head. The impact forced his upper body to pitch forwards as bone fragments and brains burst from the front of his skull and he fell on me. Brody pushed him with his boot and the cannibal slumped onto the area carpet beside me, arms spread with the knife still in his hand.

Brody put two more bullets into him, toppled into the fridge, and then slid down onto his ass. "I've lost a lot of blood..."

"My hands!" I called frantically, pulling on the rope. "You need to untie my hands, baby!"

"Baby... I like that." He smiled somewhat and said evenly, "Hold your hands as far apart as possible."

Before I could get 'why?' out of my mouth, he'd fired the gun at the thick knot. The bullet cut enough of the rope that I was able to twist my right hand free.

~

I DID the best I could with the medical supplies we had. I removed three slugs from Brody's shoulder, hip, and thigh, and I stitched several deep gashes that looked as if they'd been inflicted by a scythe blade. He was barely lucid as I bathed and dressed him before helping him out to the truck. I loaded Mr. McMurty's pickup with our duffel bag and a plastic bag full of food from the fridge. Per Brody's instructions, I drove through the night—two hundred and fifty miles northeast—and checked in to a five-star hotel at the outskirts of the city. We ditched the truck at an abandoned factory and removed the license plates.

Brody didn't have to say it. We were heading straight back into the lion's den so he could wipe out End Life. Jack had forced his hand. My life was in constant peril, and he wanted to be with me, so he made the decision to stop the rot at its source. Otherwise, we'd never be free.

It felt nice to sleep in a queen-size bed with a goose down duvet—a luxurious treat. Our suite had everything: sunken tub with jets, satellite TV with all the porn stations, room service, even a fully stocked bar. We spent weeks eating, fucking, and sleeping.

Propped against several pillows, ashtray in my lap, I leisurely sucked on a cigarette, pressing the remote. "Soon as I'm done smoking, I'll rewrap your wounds."

"Thank you." Brody suddenly sat next to me and I caught a whiff of peanut butter.

I noticed the open jar. "Not this again!" I whined. He came closer while I moved the ashtray and leaned sideways, squinting to avoid contact. "Okay, you've got a weird fetish. Did you suffer some peanut butter trauma as a kid, or what?"

He completely ignored me, dug inside the jar, and hooked a fingertip of peanut butter. I tried not to crack a smile as he smeared it on my lips. "Seriously, this is sick," I said through my teeth, mashing out my cigarette. He grinned, pinched my chin, and his eyes twinkled with naughtiness, like a child caught with his hand in the cookie jar. "And it's chunky."

He sucked on his finger then licked the corner of my mouth.

"Oh come on!" I protested with anxious, giddy laughter, grabbing his forearms. "Do you want to sniff my ass next?"

"Maybe."

"I should mark my territory, too, then."

"Be my guest." He tore open his shirt, and I was giggling.

With all our movement, the ashtray fell on the floor with a thud.

He licked me clean of the peanut butter, we made love in the missionary position on the bed, and by midnight I was done— zapped of all energy. His stamina was phenomenal considering that his wounds were still healing.

Then he fell asleep beside me, his breathing heavy. I doused my cigarette and set the ashtray on the nightstand. Got comfortable and affectionately stroked his thick, soft hair like a cat would knead a blanket. I was enraptured by the man, totally taken in by his unusual behavior and what I could only describe as his idea of undying love. He was faithful, considerate, and supportive, strange for a killer. But then maybe I was the strange one.

Whatever, we'd shared a memorable evening. My worry was that it would be one of our last. Once he confronted End Life, there'd be no turning back. I didn't know what I would do without him.

APPRENTICE KILLERS

Book Four

AUTHOR'S NOTE

Apprentice Killers is the fourth book in my Reaper series. This time evil monozygotic twins Bertram and Earnest Ballard, inseparable since birth, confront Brody. I've always been fascinated by twins—how in a majority of cases they share a near-psychic link and an unbreakable spiritual bond. Whether the situation is good, bad, or ugly, they seem committed to protecting each other no matter the consequences. And my characters are no different, except their connection isn't healthy, for obvious reasons. Feeding off one another's sadistic energy, Bertram and Earnest love to toy with their victims. Their names were inspired by a famous television duo. Can you guess which?

CHAPTER ONE

The incursion of summer brought with it blistering heat. The air hung stale and dead. Sweat beaded my brow and trickled to the base of my spine whenever I dared to move. My shirt, despite the fact that it was an airy cotton, still stuck to me like plastic wrap over a bowl of leftovers. I felt confined. I wanted to live naked, as nature intended, free of material constraint. But if I did that, there was no telling how Brody would react. He'd become just as much a sexual predator as he was a serial killer.

The large umbrella overhead blocked the direct sunlight from my upper body, but my bare legs were exposed from the knees down. There wasn't so much as a whisper of a breeze, which made me sluggish. I lit a cigarette and slouched against the circular table, resting my chin on the heel of my palm while the smoke rose like fluid in motion through my eyelashes. Lips parched and throat scratchy dry, I sucked on the warm filter and listened to the sizzle of tobacco, the commotion in the street briefly drawing my gaze.

Of all the hotels and motels we'd stayed at, this was the first with a balcony, so I took the opportunity to get a little fresh air and catch up on my reading. And *Jane Eyre*, a prolix piece of mid-nineteenth-century fiction that I never would've chosen had it not been for Brody, was spread open on the café-size table in front of me. He said if I wanted to broaden my horizons, I had to make allowances. Thrillers and fantasies were great, but there was more to the literary world.

"You're still engrossed."

I glanced at him, a dull silhouette between the open French doors. "It's kind of boring."

"I thought you would've consumed the mere five hundred pages by now."

He grinned and I chuckled, closing the book. "Not too likely. My speed has improved, but I still prefer to take my time so I really understand what I'm reading."

"That is preferable."

"I'm thirsty. Would you like a cool drink?" Keeping my fingers on the closed book, I got up from the table.

"That would be nice." He sat down to wait for me.

I returned in seconds and handed him a chilled beer from the bar fridge. "You promised to tell me about the 'list.'"

He examined the can of beer. "The list is comprised of names divided into two groups: 'confirmed' and 'potential'—as in potential candidates for the Snuff program. After my induction, I completed my training with few issues. Then, like Jack and Maxine, I became a confirmed asset."

"Where does End Life find a 'potential?'"

He snapped open the tab on his can and his gaze drifted to the street below. "Trials."

"Oh, I get it. They watch the media, and when a killer is apprehended, they step in."

"Only if the killer possesses specific behavioral traits." He sipped his beer.

"You mean like a sociopath?"

"Selection is based on emotional quotient."

"I'm sorry...?"

"The level of a person's emotional intelligence." He leaned

forwards with his elbows on his knees. "Maxine was abused sexually by her older brother."

The information itself didn't really come as a surprise; Maxine had abhorred men. "How do you know that?"

"The psychiatric records."

I thought about what Brody had told me once: for him, everything was black and white, cut-and-dried. And he didn't do anything without a good reason. "You snooped," I said with slight astonishment. "So you knew they'd send Maxine after you. And the only way to combat the enemy is to understand the enemy."

"Yes."

"Now I'm even more curious. Tell me everything."

Brody sighed. "Doctor Günter, a German psychiatric scientist, is the head of the Snuff program. Whomever the government deemed expendable, I was ordered to kill. Doctor Günter believed that if the person deserved to die—under his advisement—the program's orders would satisfy my sense of logic as well as my need to kill. He also believed he'd trained me to obey his authority no matter his decision. But I never was satisfied. I prefer to choose my own targets."

"You're a free spirit," I said. He grinned. He liked my analogy, and I smiled then polished off my beer. "What about Maxine?"

"The abuse started when she was six. Her older brother molested her. When she told her parents, her father beat her severely for lying and her mother withdrew to another bottle of scotch." He stared into the distance, his hands lightly clasping the can between his legs. He looked good: short-sleeved shirt exposing his lean, muscular arms, long black hair, and no glasses. "She ran away at seventeen, met a man who raped her, and she killed him in a frenzied attack with a pair of scissors. She'd become a byproduct of her upbringing. Once she realized she had the capacity to murder, her fear of the opposite sex vanished and her killing spree began. Eighteen victims later, three of which were her parents and brother, she ended up on death row."

"Then End Life intervened."

"Yes."

"What about Jack?" I lit a cigarette and tucked the lighter in my pocket.

"Jack was different. He was born into an impoverished family from the south—wheat farmers. As you already know, he too was on trial for murder when End Life stepped in. Due to insufficient patient history and Jack's uncooperative nature, the court appointed physiatrist concluded that he was born with his abhorrent fetish. She believed it to be a mental disorder."

"But you believe otherwise?"

"I lived with Jack for over a decade. He met a gay anthropophagite at fifteen. Jack didn't give details, but I deduced from our conversations that he'd admired the man and they'd shared an intimate relationship. The man had taught him. Therefore the consumption of human flesh was a learned trait, a product of like minds."

Fiddling with my cigarette, I felt compelled to ask. "Aside from those two fuckers, who are thankfully dead, is there anyone else on the list who could come after us?"

He was quiet and reflective for a moment then said with gravity, "The Ballard twins."

Brody had mentioned once that he'd had a twin, a duplicate of himself who hadn't survived birth. I wondered: if his brother were alive, would they be kindred spirits filled with the lustful craving for blood. And when I looked at Brody, I suspected he was thinking the same thing. "So there are others who completed the training."

"Possibly."

"Well, either they did or didn't." Irritated, I took a drag and dropped the butt inside my beer can. A last wisp of smoke escaped from the pear-shaped hole.

"The twins were enlisted only a week before I met you."

"Okay, but you must know something."

"Minimal information."

"Then make an educated guess." I walked into our suite and removed my damp T-shirt, which I threw at a garbage bag full to bursting with dirty laundry.

He suddenly hugged my waist from behind, and the heat of his breath on my neck made me shudder with excitement. I closed my eyes, holding his forearms as he whispered in my ear. "Bertram and his younger brother Earnest have an incestuous relationship. They had their first sexual encounter on the Ferris wheel in their hometown amusement park. Which Bertram instigated during puberty. Their parents blamed raging hormones. Both tested for higher than normal levels of testosterone. But Bertram also has a fixation with his brother. He believes that in order for them to remain together forever, they must be united in mind, body, and soul."

"Are you worried?" I asked, glancing at him from the corner of my eye.

"Bertram is immature and reckless." He kissed the crease of my mouth.

"So that's a n-no," I stuttered.

"I am a veteran."

His hand slid inside the front of my shorts, and I groaned. He teased my damp cock, his fingers lightly pinching the base. Lately, every time we had sex he tried something different. It was as if he was testing me.

"Jack liked to...screw his meal first. Maxine had the same preference, but she didn't eat anyone, and now you say the Ballard twins share an immoral relationship. It sounds to me all your co-workers have some type of sexual perversion."

"Most killers do." He held my wrist and led me toward the bed.

"Then what's yours?"

With the curtains closed, only his razor-sharp grin was visible in the half-cut daylight. "Isn't it obvious?"

"Not really." The insinuation was clear, but I wanted to hear him say it.

"I feel nothing sexual whatsoever when I kill. But when it

comes to you I am continually in rut, and that's what gives me a rush."

This whole thing with End Life had been a game to him. It was useful only because it gave him free rein to do as he saw fit. But when the company involved me, it forced him to protect me, and that's what gave him sexual gratification. Every time something happened, he'd get turned on and we'd have sex.

Holy shit. Why didn't I notice it sooner?

"It is simple. You are the deciding factor, Zeus. If you're hurt, I get excited because it gives me an excuse to do what I do best. But don't misinterpret. I don't wish to see you come to harm."

"God. You mean....*sexually* excited." I collapsed on the bed as he gently pushed my chest.

"My perversion lies in you."

"You see me as helpless?"

"More or less." He kissed my chin, pulling my shorts down past my hips.

"What if I started to kill too?" I touched his hair as he kissed my belly.

"The idea does have potential. Perhaps I'd become more impassioned. Although it's doubtful, considering I prefer a weak lover."

"Have you had others?" Truthfully, I didn't *want* to know if he'd slept with someone else—just the thought gave me mild chest pains. But I *had* to know. It was as if I had to be better than whoever had come before me.

"One."

"Girl or...?"

"A boy."

"You *are* gay, then."

"It would seem so."

"How long were you together?"

He blinked and his gaze went from cold to burning with desire. I knew what was to come and willingly spread my legs. "Seven and a half months. He was a classmate. We were quite demonstrative with one another. I was sixteen; he was a year older.”

“I bet you dominated the relationship.” I tensed, biting the inside of my lip as the swollen head of his cock pressed on my anus.

“He didn’t mind. He was meek.”

CHAPTER TWO

*M*eek. That word ran through my mind repeatedly while we had sex. Then it preoccupied my thoughts as we ate dinner. I hated it. The adjective trampled my pride as a man and implied I was submissive. I'd spent almost my entire life subservient to others, and there was no way I'd let it continue now.

Squeezing my fork and knife, I stopped eating. "I'm not meek," I snapped. "He may have been, but I'm not. And I'm not helpless, either."

Brody's steely gaze connected with mine, and I looked at my plate, afraid to tell him how I really felt.

"That's why you didn't enjoy the sex. I wondered."

"Well, I don't like the comparison...whoever he was."

"Understood."

"Is that all you have to say?" I set my utensils down.

"At this moment, you will perceive anything I say as derogatory."

"Is it so bad that I want you to respect me for whom I am?"

"No." He straightened, resting his forearms in his lap with an unreadable expression—stoic as usual.

I sighed, flopped backward into my chair, and scratched my

scalp; my head hurt. There were times when I had no patience for his insensitivity. "Whatever. It doesn't matter. Forget I said anything."

"I was tactless. Forgive me. I do care about you, Zeus."

That was about as close to an apology as I'd get. But it worked; he'd subdued the beast. Standing beside the table, I leaned down and kissed his forehead. "Thanks."

After that we strolled in the nearby woods as the setting sun spread dusky oranges and fiery fuchsias across the horizon like dye through water. When darkness fell, we stopped in a glade with a clear view of the city.

"The lights make it look pretty. I wish I had a camera."

"Agreed."

WE'D BEEN STAYING in various hotels on the outskirts of the city under the assumption End Life would make a move. But nothing had happened since the spring, and it was late August now. It seemed we were forgotten. Even Mr. McMurty's murder went unreported, as I never read anything in the newspapers. Maybe Brody's manipulative trainers had decided to give up. At least that's what I'd presumed until the next morning, when a woman from reception delivered a plain envelope with only three words scrawled on the front: *To the Prodigy*.

Brody sliced the envelope then set the knife on the counter. The message inside was also three words: *We found him*. Letters cut from a magazine and glued to cream notepaper. Quite cliché. It showed a lack of imagination. I'm not sure what effect the twins desired, but they got one. Scrunching the message, Brody clenched his jaw. Ninety-nine percent of the time he was calm, but there was the odd instance when he lost his composure and the gleam in his eyes turned deadly. I flinched as a chair swept through the air and bashed the far wall.

"I don't despise my parents." Once again, he appeared composed, pushing his glasses up his nose.

"I never said you did."

"My father is a kind man."

Surprised, I lit a cigarette and wandered outside onto the patio to sit at the table. Brody rarely complimented anyone. Perhaps they'd shared a close relationship. "What does this have to do with your old man?"

"The 'him' in the message is in all likelihood a reference to my father."

"You mean...they've gone after him."

"Aside from you and my father, I care for no one."

I examined my cigarette and took another, deeper drag, savoring the peace it gave me. Then I snuffed its existence in the ashtray. "How do we find out if your father is okay?"

"I will go home." He gripped the rail and leaned forwards slightly, his attention on the city. "I won't ask you to accompany me this time."

"Why not?"

"Someone will be there waiting for me. Whoever it is will target you. I won't risk a repeat of what happened with Jack and Maxine."

"That may be so, but it's not for you to decide!"

"The closer we get to End Life, the more perilous the confrontations will become."

The metal chair legs scraped the tile as I rose to stand in front of him. Even with the glasses on, he had a baby face. It reminded me of the first time we'd met, when he'd charmed his way into my psyche with a barrage of terse intellect. At first I was in awe. Then he bewitched me. Raising my hand, I touched his smooth, warm cheek—not what you'd expect from a cold, calculating man.

"You're my world...and my everything. I don't care what they throw at us, I will be with you until the end."

His eyes were intent, relentless in their search for whatever made me tick. Whenever I threw my emotions at him, he dissected them, endeavoring to understand. He had a torrid soul, one that strived for release and humanity, and I could see it every time I looked into his steely-gray gaze. And it was that gaze that held my happiness. At least I meant something to someone.

"I really love you, Brody. You're the only good I have in this world. If you leave me now...I won't make it."

His fingers sank into my hair and he drew me close and kissed my forehead, wrapping me in a secure embrace. I shut my eyes and smiled—the tears fell without warning—and I slid my hands around his back. The faint, comforting scent of shaving lotion and body heat was in his shirt, signaling his presence.

WE WOKE EARLY, packed, and ate breakfast in the hotel restaurant. Then we rode local transit to a used car lot west of the hotel. Brody paid a couple thousand in cash for a mid-sized maroon truck. The truck was pretty beat up, and with a quarter million miles registered on the odometer, I was surprised it ran. But it was a cheap and inconspicuous set of wheels.

I'd always wondered where Brody got his seemingly never-ending stream of money. That day, during the drive, he told me End Life had paid them to kill. Substantial government funds backed not only the program but every participant who became an asset as well. He'd drained his wages from the bank and put them into a different account via an international financial institute. He'd set up the account under an alias—his long-dead boyfriend's name. His parents had also given him a trust fund, which he'd transferred into that same account. He had ID under the boy's name. Money was wired from the international account to a dummy account and finally withdrawn in cash—by someone else—and put into a safety deposit box, the location of which he wouldn't reveal. The only other person with access to his finances was a retired attorney, friend of his father, who would take care of things in the event of Brody's death.

Brody drove for the first leg of our journey, and I took over when darkness fell. By the time the sun peeked over the horizon, I'd driven to the edge of the state, far from the city.

I pressed on the brake and the truck came to a rocky stop with dust sweeping past. The radio crackled with country music from a local station until there was a click, and the music died. Brody was awake, his fingers releasing the volume knob. I held the steering wheel with both hands: ten and two o'clock. The sign a few yards ahead read *Golden Valley. Pop. 7,000.*

The view was spectacular from the knoll. Undulating downwards and beyond was a wide valley blanketed in a patchwork quilt of yellows, purplish-blue, green, and brown, with a road eroded by weather cutting straight through the center. A hundred-year-old split-rail fence lined either side of the ditches that separated the farm land from the asphalt. Brody said the canola and alfalfa would be ready for harvest toward fall, and their rich scents were in the breeze. Brody also mentioned it was typical prairie weather for the summer. The sun was baking hot and the skies the purest of blue with the odd, anomalous wisp of cotton-white clouds.

I'd never seen anything like it—the grandeur and space. Prostitution had once been my prison, segregating me from the rest of the world. But the more I saw of what life had to offer, the more I was thankful I'd met Brody.

"Where to?"

"Stay on this road. In three-quarters of a mile, there will be a supermarket on the right. We can get a drink."

"Okay." I put the shifter into drive and we sped off toward the heart of Golden Valley.

CHAPTER THREE

*B*rody caught a glimpse of auburn hair—sunlit hues of radiant red. The young woman held a bag of groceries to her partially exposed chest as she exited the store. She had a vivacious air, bright smile, and perky bounce in her step that caused her ponytail to swish her sun-kissed shoulders. He followed her out of the supermarket into a parking lot lined with dry grass and giant trees. Most were of the nut variety, and dehydrated seed-pods littered the ground.

He sat on a wood bench, slats faded where the lacquer had rubbed off. Screwed to the backrest was a dedication plaque in oxidized brass that read, 'In loving memory of Sadie Ketchum.' He wondered briefly who Sadie Ketchum was when he noticed subtle movement in his peripheral. "I knew a girl similar in appearance," he said.

The young woman got into a compact, blue, European-model car.

"When was that?" Zeus sat down on his right, dropped a bag of groceries between his runners, and lit a cigarette.

"High school."

"I get the feeling your memories aren't pleasant."

"Jessica Humboldt was a remarkable bully."

"God, I can't *stand* bullies." Zeus flicked ash at the ground and took another drag.

"Don't misconstrue my choice of adjective. I despise those who prey on the weak. But her strength of purpose fascinated me."

"Well, good. For a moment there I thought you'd gone soft on me."

He noted the mordant ring in his lover's tone; Zeus was evolving. The more confidence he acquired the more openly he spoke his mind. He watched the blue car merge into the traffic. "She believed her superior intellect gave her privilege, and she turned humiliation into an art form. She could pinpoint her victim's Achilles' heel. It was the leverage she used to terrorize."

Zeus looked at him. "So what did she do to you?"

The question didn't catch him off-guard, however, it did trigger a physical response. He felt an ache in the center of his chest that he could only associate with an emotional loss. He'd experienced it just once before. "It isn't *what* she did, it's *who* she did it to."

BRODY BLINKED SLOWLY, and when he opened his eyes the environment around him had changed. He was in the second floor hallway of his high school, and a girl with the same auburn hair was inside a nearby classroom. Jessica's expression wasn't congenial like the smile of the woman from the supermarket; instead her mouth was curled in a vicious snarl. The girl seated in front of her covered her face with her hands. Over a period of two semesters, he'd watched Jessica systematically torment a number of students both male and female.

Jessica yelled and slapped the girl. Teary-eyed, the girl slid her tremulous hands higher, shielding her head. The others teenagers in the classroom feigned ignorance. They looked out the windows, buried their heads in books, or continued to eat their lunch. No one dared to get involved. Brody didn't feel anything in particular for the victim. But he felt something simmering deep within for the bully.

Rising from his slouched position against the wall, he stared at Jessica. When she noticed him, she froze with her fist in the air, and her already stern lip line soured to that of aversion. She grabbed her knapsack and burst into the hallway. As he knew she would, she'd come to meet him head-on. The coldness in her glare told him everything, but he wasn't fazed. Again, his mind elicited no emotional response. And his heart continued to beat at a relaxed and steady rate.

"You'd better mind your own business, geek." She jerked her thumb toward the classroom. "If not, you'll get worse than she did."

"Prepare yourself," he said evenly.

She stopped dead in the middle of the hallway and after a moment's pause turned around. "What the fuck did you say?"

Everyone in the classroom watched, their curiosity growing by the second.

"To simplify: you don't scare me. Threaten her once more and I will kill you."

She didn't move, and she didn't show any obvious signs of fear. However, he did observe a slight tremble in her hand as her grip tightened on her knapsack strap, and her pupils dilated. He sensed a rise in her pulse and a hesitation to react. She was terrified and debating her odds.

Sliding his hands into his hip pockets, he bent closer and flashed a grin. "I can see straight through you, bitch."

She leaned backward, trepidation growing in her eyes, and nervously barked, "If you know what's good for you you'll just stay the fuck away from me, asshole!"

He watched as she strode to the end of the hallway and descended a wide set of steps.

ZEUS BENT FORWARDS, dropped his butt, and mashed it under the grinding pressure of his shoe. "I'm guessing she didn't stop after that."

"The trouble escalated. The only deduction I could make was that she'd seen us together."

"Us?"

"Cody and I."

"I take it he was the high school boyfriend."

"Yes."

THE LOCATION once again switched in Brody's mind. He'd returned to his childhood home, and the images were as vivid and real as if he'd stepped back in time. His parents were seated at the dining room table, an extended rectangle of mahogany that could easily accommodate an additional nine guests.

"I'm gay," he said. He saw no reason to hide his sexuality.

As the initial shock began to wear off, his mother's mood plunged into darkness. She grabbed the glass in front of her and gulped a mouthful of wine. His father set his fork and knife on his dinner plate and sat back, exhaling a sigh like the hiss of a deflating balloon.

He could've changed his mind right then and put his mother at ease with a few simple lies, but he could never fool his father. Florence wasn't gullible, but she was too trusting. Richard, on the other hand, had a straightforward, mechanical way of thinking. He was a surgeon, highly intelligent and not easily fooled.

"Do you understand the implications of what you just said?" Richard asked.

"I do."

"Why men?" Florence searched his eyes, her voice frosty and acrimonious. "You're so clever and attractive."

"Intelligence and appearance don't dictate a person's sexuality."

"But I want grandchildren..." Her features were strained as if she could scarcely breathe; she placed her arms on the table and made a fist. "I'd hoped you would graduate...find a good girl and get married."

"You're worried about what everyone else will think."

"Of course I am. People can be cruel—life can be cruel! No one will accept a homosexual relationship. My God, Brody, what the hell are you thinking?"

Richard touched her wrist, but she snatched her arm away as if bitten and stood, rattling the dinnerware. Moments later a door in the outer hallway slammed.

Neither he nor his father spoke.

He felt it necessary to prepare his parents, because Cody was Jessica's newest target, and eventually their relationship would be brought to light.

Brody blinked. He was back in school, and a month had passed. The bell rang, signaling a class change. The doors opened and a flood of bodies crowded the hallway, voices and confusion everywhere. Cody was walking quickly in his direction, his jacket and shirt wet and his complexion noticeably flushed. Brody shut his locker and went to say something, but his lover rushed past with watery eyes, pushing through the people. Brody knew Cody desired comfort, but was too ashamed to ask. And his peers—a small group of mindless peons under Jessica's thumb—were watching.

He noted the exit Cody took. The other boys permitted him a wide berth. In fact, the oncoming wave thinned as students hastily backed out of Brody's way. No one spoke, but everyone watched intently. The harassment had worsened. Brody didn't care who knew about their relationship, but he did care about Cody.

CHAPTER FOUR

Cody's strawberry blond hair sparkled with a hint of honey in the sunlight. But his sallow features were damp with tears, his brow was furrowed, and the painful truth of harassment showed in his wide blue eyes. He was trying to think of a way out. Brody stood at a distance, concealed by the shadow of a large tree. Putting pressure on Cody in front of the entire school wasn't wise; he'd already reached his tipping point.

"They called me a fag in front of the whole class. Then this one big guy asked me if I liked being fucked up the ass...if I came from my ass." Cody gulped, keeping his back to the classroom windows, pressing his forearm to his stomach. "When I ignored him, these two other guys threw chocolate milk at me and said since I liked to have my fudge packed I should look like it."

"Take a deep breath."

"I'm not you," Cody cried, squeezing his fist.

"That isn't what I meant. Sorry."

"It's what they do to me when you're not looking. I'm really scared, Brody."

Brody scanned the windows. Classes were in session, giving them an audience they didn't need. "Go home."

"Huh?"

"Keep walking and don't look back. I'll be there in an hour."

"But my textbooks... I've got a test tomorrow."

"Don't worry." He flashed a smile. He couldn't prevent the stress, but he could alleviate it. "Let me protect you." His lover exhaled as if he'd been holding his breath underwater, and the tension released from his hunched shoulders. Cody nodded and disappeared from the schoolyard.

"That was cruel."

"Exceptionally."

Zeus put a cigarette in his mouth, frowned, and ignited the tip; his lover empathized with Cody. They shared similar personality traits, but the strength Cody had lacked Zeus was gradually learning to command.

"How far is it to your house from here?"

"Twenty minutes southwest of the town core."

"Okay. Since it's your turf, you can drive." Zeus tossed him the keys, picked up the bag of groceries, and walked toward the truck.

Brody caught the keys. "We'll wait until dark. Are you hungry?"

THE HOUSE LOOKED the same as it had when he was growing up: colonial white, marble pillars at the front, and tall black-shuttered windows. Upper middle class with an air of dignity. Carefully pruned trees and shrubbery and a water feature stood in the center of the gated yard. Brody unlocked the front entrance with a brass key he'd found under a large stone in the flowerbed. He gave the door a gentle push. Inside the foyer were a baby grand piano and a circular Persian carpet. An overabundance of family photos in plain frames hung on one wall beneath ten-inch crown molding. An antique mirror hung opposite, above a walnut credenza with a hand-blown vase of dead flowers.

Brody moved in silence with Zeus as his shadow. The chandelier was on; the crystals sparkled as he passed underneath.

"Your mother was a beautiful woman." Zeus looked away from the wall of family memories. "What is it?"

"Search the rest of the house." Brody drew his gun and walked past the piano into the hallway. On his immediate right was his father's study. Light shone under the heavy wood door.

He aimed while slowly turning the knob. Then he stood on the threshold, the observer to a grisly scene. Richard was seated at an oak barrister's desk, his throat slit ear to ear like a clown's hideous red smile. A note had been driven into the desktop with the murder weapon: a butcher knife, the blade glossy with dried blood. Just as he had suspected, his father was dead, likely already gone by the time he'd received the message. The floor-to-ceiling bookshelves behind Richard appeared undisturbed, but the lofty wood-framed window to the right was partially open, the pale floral sheers caught in the gap as the flow of air sucked them in and out, like a giant taking a breath. Nothing had been stolen. Everything was just as he'd remembered. His father was meticulous, and everything had its place, even the newly acquired items that he'd never seen.

His father's milky, half-lidded stare urged him closer. Keeping his hand over his father's eyes, his own vision blurred. The moisture fell from his cheek and he wiped it, examining his wet fingertips. *Is this what it means to love?* He thought about Cody, his mother, and then Zeus, the only light left in his dark world.

He said composedly, "You repaired so many broken bodies. I admired you."

"I'm so sorry, baby."

Brody's hand slipped away from his father's face as he spoke over his shoulder. "Thank you. Did you find anything?"

"Nothing." Zeus gestured to the note with a frown, his dark eyes sympathetic. "What does it say?"

"'Amusement parks are fun.'"

"I take it that's where they want to meet."

"The twins are enthusiasts." He holstered his gun and stood in front of a section of ornate wood panel—a square with elaborate, deep grooving. He pressed on the panel and opened it with a click to reveal a wall safe.

"You mean the Ferris wheel?"

"Supposedly they gave each other a hand job while necking, as the wheel rushed earthward."

"Okay. They sound like a pair of fuck-ups."

"Indeed, and dangerous."

"Is there one around here...a park?"

"Yes. It's been closed for many years."

"What do we do now?"

He opened a black velvet box and took the rings from inside: his-and-hers diamond-cut platinum bands. "We will eat and rest for the night."

"You ca-can't be serious."

He stared dead ahead, grasping the rings tighter; he knew why his lover was upset. "I take it my father's corpse makes you uncomfortable."

"Yeah, just a little. Doesn't it bother you?"

"I don't believe in ghosts," he said in monotone. "However, yes, it bothers me, because he was important to me. But since there is nothing I can do to bring him back, I must accept the situation, grim as it is, and move on."

Zeus sighed. "I'm so sorry, I didn't mean any disrespect. I guess I'm still in shock and feeling a little anxious..."

After a moment's pause, Brody said reassuringly, "The maid won't be here until Monday, and my father has no close friends that would find the absence of a phone call odd. He turned into a recluse after my mother died, refusing all invitations to social functions and community gatherings. So I believe it'll be safe to stay."

"Okay. We'll stay, I guess."

"Don't worry." He put the rings in a hip pocket of his jeans, locked the safe, and clicked the panel shut. "If you like, you can shower while I prepare something to eat."

CHAPTER FIVE

*B*rody caught a whiff of soap, the manufacturer's interpretation of how a spring day smelled. Zeus had put on a baby blue T-shirt and black sweats. He smiled to himself. As usual, his lover's fresh-from-the-shower look—damp hair and rosy complexion—gave him a hard-on. "I made grilled cheese sandwiches and tomato soup."

"I haven't had one of these in years." Zeus peeled back the top layer of fried bread and his eyes lit up. "And you made it with cheddar and mozza. This is great!"

"The correct choice, then."

"Oh yeah, I love cheese, and mixing different kinds is the best way."

He slid onto a chair at the kitchen table and watched, fascinated, as the young man devoured two sandwiches and three servings of soup in less than ten minutes.

"Aren't you going to eat?"

"I already have."

When Zeus had consumed the last morsel, he washed the dishes then hopped up to sit on the granite counter. Legs dangling, he lit a cigarette and exhaled a sated sigh. Brody read the contentment in his faint smile; Zeus really enjoyed smoking after eating.

"Thanks for making dinner." Zeus hunched, holding the ashtray in his lap.

"You're welcome."

"So, what happened that day...in high school? You never did finish your story."

He leaned forward and rested his elbows on his knees, allowing his hands to hang limp between his legs. "I'm antisocial, so high school was a nuisance. The only reason I attended was because my parents felt home schooling would only isolate me more."

"Okay, you did what your parents wanted. You were obedient."

"I had no reason to act disrespectful."

Zeus laughed, eyeing him. "Knowing you, your grades were perfect too."

"They were well above average."

"What about friends?"

"I never felt a need to cultivate friendships. Most humans are self-centered and don't care for those around them."

"That's a depressing outlook. Everyone needs companionship. We're built for it." Zeus slid off the counter with the ashtray and sat on the kitchen table directly in front of him instead.

"I told you, Zeus." He straightened. "I'm different."

"Sure, you're wired a little different from most people, but I don't think that means you want to be totally alone. You picked me, and now we're together."

Brody couldn't help but smirk. He closed his eyes as his memories came into focus. "The last day I attended school was the last time I saw Cody..."

BRODY STOOD in the open doorway of the storage portable that held an accumulation of new and old phys-ed equipment. Daylight cut around him to reveal a body on the floor. Cody was sprawled out, his lower body naked, bruised and bloody. The air stunk of piss and excrement. His lover had been severely beaten, and he wasn't moving. He noticed everything in the compact space: the dildo, rope and camera, and the uneasy expressions of his classmates.

"Oh, I get it," Jessica taunted. "You're upset, huh, you fucking fag, 'cos I messed with your lover."

Her companions: two male students, laughed mockingly.

"Well, don't worry. He isn't dead. He's just really tired from all the sex."

Even though the sight had registered, Brody still needed to process his emotions. It was the only way he'd know how to adequately respond. And the only thing he felt at that moment was a painful ache in the center of his chest. Was it love? He'd treated Cody with tenderness and done whatever the older boy had asked. Cody was a kind, good kid who adored him.

He made mental calculations: the rear exit was blocked by heavy equipment, and the grimy window was too small to climb through.

Reaching back, he slowly shut the door.

"Hey, what are you doing?" asked one boy.

"What I should've done a long time ago." He turned the deadbolt.

"Who the fuck do you think you are?" Jessica demanded.

"I told you he's a fucking psycho," the second boy retorted. "I told you to leave it alone!"

"What, are you scared now?" she sneered. "Huh? Frightened of the faggot weirdo?"

Never taking his eyes off them, Brody leaned sideways and grasped a two-foot metal pipe from a plastic crate, a piece of weight-lifting equipment that held small weights used for bicep curls. And everyone started to yell and clamber for the window.

He could feel it brewing—the storm he just barely kept under control. The blinding rage was the chink in his armor, that moment when his logic conceded to madness. It had a tantalizing quality: blood for justice.

He lunged, bludgeoning the first boy in seconds, an instant fatal blow to the temple, while the other tried frantically to get the equipment away from the rear door. But as soon as the kid sensed his presence he turned around with his hands up. "Please! I'm sorry!"

"Apology not accepted." Brody split his skull wide open.

"Go to hell, asshole!" Jessica rushed for the locked door.

"You first." He grinned and swung.

She screamed, careening backward. The window vibrated. He hit with violent precision, sucking in his breath with each strike. He walloped her arms and then her jaw. Then there was a distinctive crunch, like a coconut hitting cement. She was silent, hanging over a pommel horse, her long dark ringlets oozing. The scent of dirty steel on his skin was replaced with the overpowering metallic smell of his sadistic rampage. Blood ran down the back of his hand, webbed his fingers and dripped from the pipe. He gasped deeply then tilted his head back, closing his eyes. The kill had been quite gratifying. Much more than he ever imagined. Cody's rape had been vindicated—justice was served.

Carefully, he wrapped one of the boy's hands around the pipe and let it fall to the floor. Then he did the same to the other dead students, marking different pieces of weight-lifting gear with blood and their fingerprints. He decided to leave everything else exactly where it was—the camera and other items were evidence. If anything, the fake weapons would take time for the police to sort out and would plant the seeds of doubt. He would've made more precise plans, but working at the spur of the moment didn't allow for it.

Brody squatted beside Cody and dressed him. He slung Cody's arms over his shoulders then lifted him to his feet by his jeans. Cody murmured something in his semi-conscious state, and his head lolled as Brody dragged him out of the portable.

Cody lived with his mother in an apartment half a mile from the school. His father had abandoned them years before, preferring to live with gangs selling drugs and getting high. He spent most his life in prison. But despite being alone, broke, and young, Cody's mother cared about her son.

With Cody slung over his shoulder, Brody knocked on the apartment door. Marla answered in a long pink bathrobe, her strawberry blonde hair in rollers. Her big blue eyes widened soon as she saw her son, and she grabbed Brody's shirt, dragging him inside. "Oh my God, what happened?" She shut the door and nervously examined the blood smeared on her right hand. "What's wrong with my son?"

"Cody was raped by Jessica Humboldt and two of her male friends inside the Phys-Ed equipment portable."

"What did you say?" She gawped, her pallor increasing, and she clutched the robe at her chest.

Brody walked Cody into the small, dusty bedroom at the back of the apartment, and she quickly followed. His lover flopped onto the bed, and Brody straightened, panting. "She filmed it." He looked at her. "Three weeks ago she discovered we were dating, and she began to bully him. He said nothing to me but I could see what was going on. And today, she took her hatred too far."

Marla stared at her son, holding a shaky fist to her mouth. "What does that mean?"

Brody knew the police would arrest him eventually. The killing spree had occurred in daylight on school property, and more than likely something had been said during the filming of Cody's rape. Jessica had taken pleasure in gloating. "We shouldn't talk in front of him."

Bright sunlight poured in through the small window above the kitchen sink. The apartment was cozy and tidy, the table strewn with large textbooks. Marla worked nights as a waitress at a local bar, and during the day she studied to become a nurse. Cody was her life, and she wanted the best for him. Brody found her determination impressive—she was a good woman, like his father.

"I killed Jessica and the two other boys."

Her eyebrows pinched and she chewed on her thumb, evidently worried. Then she sprang into action and tore open the linen closet in the hallway. "The police will question me. It's best you don't tell me anything else."

He was surprised when she handed him a folded bath towel.

"Have a shower," she ordered, "and I'll get you some clean clothes. Quick!"

Water dripped from the showerhead as he put on the clothes Marla had left on the bathroom counter. He combed his hair and adjusted his glasses. He could hear the hum of the washer. When he opened the door, Cody greeted him with teary eyes. Brody took a wobbly step back as the older boy hugged him tight and sniveled into his chest.

"You saved me," Cody cried.

He held him. "There was no other option."

"I love you so much."

Brody kissed his head. "Me too," was the closest he could give to a meaningful reply. But it seemed enough for his lover; the teenager squeezed him.

"What do I say to the police?"

"Tell the truth. Recollection will come naturally. Lies are difficult to keep accurate."

"But I—"

"Did you actually see me kill them?"

Cody made reluctant eye contact. "No."

"Then you have no reason to worry." Brody kissed his lips.

Marla held out a bag filled with food and his damp clothes. "Thank you for helping my son, but you need to leave. Now."

THE ROOM WAS SUBMERGED in a gray haze, the ashtray overflowing. His lover had smoked more than usual and had poured a third drink. The bottle of whiskey burned amber in the low light.

"I've upset you."

"No, not at all." Zeus mashed out his cigarette. "I'm just stunned. The whole story is...unbelievable."

"You *are* familiar with my nature."

"Not that, Brody. I mean...I'm a little envious."

"Cody."

"Well, you clearly had a serious thing for him."

"As I do for you."

Zeus smirked, setting his lighter on the table. "So where is he?"

"Three years into my incarceration, he died."

"Oh." Zeus was quiet for a moment. "I'm sorry. That must've hurt."

"Not nearly as much as your woeful expression."

"I don't know what you're talking about." Zeus sniffed, quickly wiping his cheek, and turned to face the pantry.

"Cody doesn't compare to you."

"Oh, that was...slick." Zeus's laughter was short-lived and Brody heard the sadness in it. "You know, just once I'd like to hear how you really feel—just fucking once."

His own emotions were complex, difficult to pinpoint and understand, and not something he could easily translate into words. Zeus was important to him, an integral part of his daily life. But he acted like a vampire, sucking all the decency from Zeus, and gave nothing in return. And a vampire could only suck for so long before the host would die. He knew that if he didn't find a way to express himself, Zeus would become like him—a monster in a human shell.

"Just finish the story." Zeus filled another glass with whiskey and gulped it down.

"I don't want to cause you further distress."

"How did he die?"

He remained suspended by his thoughts for a second time before he answered, "He couldn't live without me."

"Sorry. That was insensitive of me."

"Not insensitive. Honest. I visited his grave the day before I met you. You remind me of him."

CHAPTER SIX

I was stunned as I rolled the cigarette between my thumb and index finger. "So that's why you chose me. Because I was like him."

"Yes. However, you are stronger."

We were quiet for a long time, me slouched against the wall as smoky ribbons twisted from the glowing tip of my cigarette. Brody got closer, studied my lips, then kissed me—a kiss that lingered with the moist warmth of his tongue on mine. I anxiously mashed the cigarette in the ashtray, which he took from me and set on the counter with a clatter. He pulled my track pants down past my ankles to the floor, spread my thighs, and squatted. My heart started to pound as he took my whole cock in his mouth. His blowjobs were the best. Dropping my head back, I released a tense sigh, playing with his hair. The wet heat of his mouth was velvety smooth, and as my excitement grew, it clouded my reality. I pinched my buttocks, lifting my hips to meet his face.

He pressed his hand to my chest and forced me to lie on the kitchen table. His chin nudged my hole and the tip of his tongue flicked my scrotum. Maybe he saw me as his dead boyfriend. Maybe the escalation of sexual experimentation was somehow an integration of our beings. Regardless, I knew one thing for certain. Brody was uninhibited and unembarrassed about everything he did or said. And he'd made it his top priority to satisfy me first.

"No...ah..." I gripped the edge of the table as my entire body jolted. My bare flesh slid up and down on the table, squeaking. "Brody, please..." My plea did nothing. He was determined to finish what he'd started.

Holding me stationary by my hips, he continued to slam my ass one hard thrust at a time, followed by another and another. "I love it when you beg," he growled.

I refused to admit how much I enjoyed Brody's dominance—and his long dick. The sex wasn't so much rough as it was a play to claim power, to name a victor. He owned the physical supremacy, and he wanted me to acknowledge it. He grabbed my erection and squeezed, jerking it while plunging as deep as possible inside me. I grunted with excitement, locked my calves around his waist, and clutched his neck.

Then we both were lost to the momentum of climactic pleasure. I cried out, and he exhaled a hard, husky groan.

He staggered back a step, his gaze scarcely lucid. And I lay immobile, my groin a sticky, pungent mess. I'd done nothing and, surprisingly, I was the one out of breath. I ran my fingers lightly through the cum on my stomach and licked my lips, as parched as if I'd spent days wandering the desert. I loved the feeling when I ejaculated, both the intensity of the moment and the aftermath, when the world faded to white and there was no one left but me.

He grasped my wrist to help me up from the table. Then he led me barefoot through the main floor of the house, up the stairs to the second floor, and into a dark bedroom. I was astonished when he held my face, kissed me, and said, "Let's shower and go to bed."

We'd never showered together. And when he cuddled me under the covers, my heart started to gallop like a racehorse. Bewildered by his unabashed affection, I laid rigid in his arms, wondering what the hell was going on. Maybe I'd got his intentions all wrong. Maybe he was trying to act more human to please me.

Love.

Could it be love?

The whole thing made me anxious, so I gently wiggled free of his arms. He searched my expression, questioning, and heat scored my cheeks.

"Too much?" he asked.

"I appreciate it, but...I'm just feeling a little overwhelmed right now."

"Understood." He remained on his side, facing me, his gaze unwavering. "Perhaps I should continue to tell you my story instead?"

"Yeah." I coaxed with a smile. "Please do."

He blinked, and a fragment of time he spent in jail came into focus. His wrists were handcuffed and chained to a metal table, the corners bull-nosed. Florence's dark blond hair was in a ponytail, her clothes tidy and cheerful, but her hands were weathered along with her features as she nervously twisted her wedding ring. His father was impeccably neat, tall, and wiry with cropped black hair and a cold gray stare—a carbon copy of his son. Keeping his posture rigid, Richard brought his hands together to rest on the table.

"Did you actually do what the police claim you did?" his mother asked.

He noted the glassy sheen in her eyes. She was devastated. But his father's expression was different—not angry or revolted or even disappointed. Brody saw almost a tolerant appreciation in his gaze —at least it seemed that way.

"I did."

"Oh my God." She cupped her face and bent over crying.

His father gently rubbed her back. The gesture seemed mechanical, a hollow empathy performed strictly for the sake of his mother and the policemen posted at the exit. And in that instant, Brody realized that he and his father were cut from identical cloth. How could he be so compassionate with his patients but not his wife? He'd always been a kind man, but now it was clear. The man had done everything simply out of duty, to strike an appearance of goodness in society.

"I'd like to talk to Brody alone."

After a moment, Florence dabbed under her eyes with a tissue and got up from the table. "All right." She paused next to Brody and touched his cheek with the back of her hand. "I love you so much."

"I love you too, Mother."

She nodded, waiting as one of the policeman unlocked and opened the door. When she'd gone and the door shut, his father restarted the conversation.

"Explain what happened," Richard demanded point-blank.

"Jessica ordered two of her classmates to rape my boyfriend while she filmed it. She intended to publicly humiliate him."

Richard wore a solemn frown, a sobering reminder that they were indeed one and the same. "Have you killed before?"

Brody looked him straight in the eyes. "No."

"Will you kill again?"

"In all probability, if necessary."

"Then you believe your actions were justified."

"I do."

His father sighed and a hint of a smile fractured his grim lip line like a crack in a mirror. "Then there's nothing more for me to say. You've made your decision."

"That is cold. I am *your* son." He grimaced, clenching his fist, trying to understand his father's lack of sympathy.

"Don't get the wrong idea, son. I love you, and I don't want to see you in jail. But we both know why you did this. Cody was just the catalyst. If it wasn't him, it would've been someone else, eventually." Richard placed his hand over his son's fist. "Whatever happens from this moment on, make sure your choices are the correct ones. The public doesn't like a vigilante, but they will tolerate him if his actions are justified."

He was stunned as his father rose from the chair.

"We can't come to your trial, for obvious reasons. But your mother and I will support you in any other way we can."

"I understand. What about a lawyer?"

"Of course."

"I'M NOT a vigilante but something far worse. My father never permitted the latter prospect to enter his mind. To him I was an anti-hero."

"Interesting concept. He believed you were justified."

Zeus straddled his lap, his cock hard again. Brody smiled and touched the glossy, wet slit. Zeus moaned softly, and he rubbed it slightly harder. "Pre-cum. You are extremely eager."

"I want you to fuck me all night."

The sex was gratifying, but he hungered for more. The lure of death was calling. Standing at the window, Brody pushed aside one of the heavy curtain panels. Moonlight obscured the night sky, and his family's estate, buffeted by woodlands behind the house, was a burnt green. Beyond that was where he needed to be. He peered over his shoulder. Zeus was sound asleep.

He thought about the twins and faced the window again. Doctor Günter assumed the manipulative Bertram was the mastermind because he possessed the brains. However, it was Earnest who rode on an uneven keel.

Images flashed, another concentrated outpouring of memories, the nature of which he wanted to erase.

HE'D JUST FINISHED a training exercise: hand-to-hand combat. He'd completed the program numerous times. It was a way to keep in shape and the road to achieving perfection. The fire exit shut behind him, and one of the florescent lights blinked. The corridor to the apartment complex was quiet. Until he reached the end. On the other side of the second door was a large change room with an open shower, lockers, benches, and toilets. The door was ajar. Voices echoed faintly and he paused, nudging it open. He knew little about the Ballard twins, who were newcomers to the Snuff program. But as he watched, he learned more than he cared to.

Earnest had his older brother pinned to the floor. Bertram's clothes were torn, his eyes watery, and his skin red like they'd just had a scrap. Earnest forcibly pried his bare thighs apart, leaned down, and licked his stiff cock to the engorged bell.

"No! Stop it, idiot!" Bertram pinched his knees and slapped Earnest.

"If you don't let me fuck you, I'll kill everyone in the complex."

"And I told you, if you do that we'll be sent back to prison."

Earnest grabbed his brother's jaw, looked him in the eyes, and growled like a dog. "You know what'll happen if I'm locked up. So be a good boy, Bertie."

The dynamic between the pair wasn't what Doctor Günter thought. Although Bertram matched his brother's propensity for violence with intellect, he lacked the control.

CLOSING THE CURTAIN, Brody drifted through the dark and silently closed the bedroom door.

CHAPTER EIGHT

He stood stationary, the grass soft as mohair underfoot, and the cool breeze caressing his face. The backyard was the same as he remembered, its manicured lawn extending to a government-protected greenbelt. He could see his mother with her easel, painting in the shade of a walnut tree next to the high stone wall masked with clematis. Flowers would be in bloom everywhere, and her cat Felix would be hiding among the perennials, squinting, his black coat sleek in the sun.

Brody was armed with only his Berettas in their black leather holsters. He wanted as much freedom of movement as possible, so he wore minimal clothing: a dull green T-shirt, faded blue jeans, and navy runners.

He needed to be on the north side of the greenbelt. He checked his wristwatch then walked straight across several acres. At the edge of the property, he climbed over a white slat fence. The forest was an inky void stretching outside his visual range.

Then he vanished, trudging deep into the void until eventually he heard the trickle of water and caught the pungent scent of skunk cabbage. He'd reached the miry edge of a creek and didn't have much farther to go. His runners sank in the damp earth as he clambered over a fallen tree. Another twenty minutes and the forest opened to a dry stretch of field—and the skeletal remains of the Golden Valley Amusement Park. It had closed the year of his incarceration, and the bankrupt owners had left everything to rot.

Brody paused to focus on the crescent-shaped sign above the main gates. He was certain that on the other side of the wrought-iron scrolls, Bertram and Earnest were waiting. But he also sensed something else, something that lingered just beyond his view.

Guns drawn, he entered the park. He studied his surroundings carefully—a collage of blackened metal jabbing the silk mantle of midnight blue sky—a familiar place that echoed with images from the past. He could smell fresh buttered popcorn and feel the gritty, gauzy stickiness of cotton candy on his fingers. He heard the music, the laughter of children and screams of joy, and he watched entranced as Cody smiled from the merry-go-round.

Then the memories were gone, and he was standing in the open. If he didn't stay alert, the consequences would be dire. He had to stop dwelling on the past. He couldn't even understand why he *was* dwelling on it. Did Cody's untimely death bother him that much? What did he feel, if anything? Regret? Guilt? He grimaced. He had to win. Zeus was the present. Zeus was all that mattered.

Canvas flapped in the wind. The tents were stained, torn, discolored, and partially deflated. The largest had collapsed from the center out, like a rotting pumpkin. And most of the vendors' huts were boarded up. He holstered the guns and searched around the base of the main tent; a hard, tubular object was sticking out of the parched grass. He clawed at the crumbling soil, yanked a section of pipe from the ground, and stood, wiping dirt from its length.

How nostalgic. He grinned.

Suddenly there was a sizzle overhead, the buzz of electricity, and the park exploded with light and noise. The old strings of bulbs glowed, and the grind of carnival music crackled in the air. Rides came alive, and the horses on the merry-go-round floated stiffly up and down.

Brody slowed his breathing, a conscious response to the inevitable. As he continued to walk, he allowed the pipe to slip a few inches through his fingers before retightening his grip. When he reached the middle of the park, Bertram and Earnest appeared directly in front of him, only half a dozen yards away.

Their clothes were identical: military fatigue shirts and shorts in blotchy blacks and grays, boots, and black socks. Their dark hair was brush-cut. They'd even camouflaged their faces. The one on the left had a compound crossbow in hand, while his twin had a sniper rifle.

"I'm Bertram."

"I'm Earnest."

"I *am* aware." He made expeditious calculations, which included mental aptitude. "It would seem that Doctor Günter has, once again, underestimated my resolve."

"You think we can't handle you." Bertram rested the loaded crossbow on his shoulder. "While you've been away playing house with the whore, we've completed some serious training. Doctor Günter underestimates no one." He gave a nod. "And what's with that little pipe?"

"I enjoy changing my modus operandi. It makes the kill all the more fun."

"Whatever. It's useless against a bow or gun."

"Yeah, it's useless."

Bertram cuffed his brother in the chest, scowling. "I told you before, haven't I? Don't repeat every single thing I say."

Earnest looked at the ground, his ears turning red, as he gripped the rifle.

Brody discerned Earnest's flaw: he wasn't able to do anything without his brother's blessing; he watched Bertram's every move and only reacted after his brother did. Brody now knew for certain that once the weaker link was broken, the other would quickly become unhinged. "The last time I killed was a pimp in Newbury two months ago," Brody said, cracking his neck. "No quarter will be given."

Bertram flung his head back in laughter. "Doctor Günter was right. You are fearless! I'm so excited now. Finally. Someone we can fight."

The noise died, and the amusement park again disappeared in the pitch black. Brody instinctively dove to the right just as a bullet grazed his cheek. His flesh burned as he landed, chest first, in the dirt. Another punched through a gaming shack, and the painted exterior wall exploded. He heard Earnest lock in the bullet chamber before taking the shot. He shielded his face and quickly crawled away to squat behind the shack. A huge slug obliterated the rough wood panel a foot from his shoulder. He flinched, ducking as debris flew. The guy was a first-rate marksman.

Listening for movement, he turned his head to the side. Footsteps approached. He dashed for the adjacent shack and slid the pipe into his belt. He drew the gun from under his left arm and peered around the building. He waited until a dark blob—Earnest—was in his sight. He went to shoot, but hesitated. In a flash, he'd calculated every possible scenario. He had a theory, but in order to test it, he had to make the first move.

Cat and mouse, he thought as he aimed and squeezed the trigger. The gunshot rang off the buildings. Earnest returned fire, and at virtually the same instant an arrow pierced Brody's arm from behind.

He stifled a groan, and as he ran toward the small roller coaster, he twisted and fired in Bertram's general direction. Earnest shot back. A bullet tore through a post. He ducked behind one of the bucket-like seats. He had to remove the arrow. Only a couple yards away were a food truck and a covered eating area, and beyond that the haunted house. But he had to cross a wide open space to get to it.

He smirked to himself. *How inconvenient.*

Just as he was about to move, someone switched the power back on. Although annoying and momentarily distracting, the commotion had its advantages. He used the roller coaster as a barrier for as long possible before he crossed the open stretch, passed the food truck, and darted inside the haunted house.

He pushed through swinging doors, snaking hallways, and mirrored walls. Ghoulish figures jumped into his path. Holding the arrow, he dodged every one, to prerecorded screams of fright. He stopped in the chamber of horrors with its tortured, mutilated dummies, their guts spilled. Red lights dimmed then flared to a bright glow at timed intervals, revealing a different section of the macabre exhibit.

It reminded him of his childhood, when Florence took him to see the large display window of a department store at Christmas. Just not as festive. He wandered into the French execution chamber and noticed a pair of pliers. Leaning his shoulder against the blackened back wall, he clamped the front section of the shaft with the pliers. Then clenching his teeth, he slowly fed the carbon arrow out of his arm. The fletching burned as it ripped all the way through his already damaged flesh, and he nearly passed out. Breathing shallow, he rested his head, the guillotine coming in and out of focus as the pliers slipped from his hand.

CHAPTER NINE

Clutching a pillow, I rolled over to find the other side of the bed unusually cold, with no warm body to snuggle into. I opened my eyes, expecting that Brody had migrated to the edge of the mattress, but he hadn't. He was nowhere to be seen. The curtains were open a slit, and the darkness around me was empty. His glasses were on the nightstand. Anxious fear gripped my heart. I quickly flung the blanket aside and bounced off the bed, scrambling to locate my clothes.

He'd gone to fight the twins.

While zipping my fly, I saw a baseball bat mounted on the wall, the aluminum handle wrapped in black tape. I grabbed it before leaving the room.

I exited the house through the rear French doors, crossing a patio laid with flagstones. Flies circled the bright exterior lights. Honestly, I had no idea where Brody was. I had to rely solely on the pittance of information he'd given me and intuition. Then I noticed footprints leading away from the patio, faint impressions in the grass. In the distant darkness past the backyard, I could just make out trees. So that's where I ran.

At the edge of the property, I climbed a fence, and without

looking back, I swallowed my apprehension and allowed the forest to take me. Like wading into the depths of a cold, bottomless lake, I felt for anything to guide me as I stepped unsteadily forward.

Soon my pupils adjusted, I became part of a whole new world. I could distinguish between various shades of black, from the trees to the rocky soil and underbrush. About fifteen minutes in, I trod in mud, and water rushed past the soles of my shoes. After that I emerged from the woods to the squeaky grind of a Ferris wheel in motion, and the music and lights of a rundown amusement park.

I wanted to call out for Brody, but I knew it wouldn't be smart. So, squeezing my chest through a broken section of fence, I snuck onto the grounds and crawled under an old fortune-telling caravan. I slid over the front axle and hunched, hanging onto the front stairs.

BRODY CAME TO. The guillotine was right in front of him, and so was Earnest, slinking into a medieval castle dungeon. He was searching. Brody sank backward into obscurity behind a figure of an executioner. He could shoot. *There's no satisfaction in that.* He grinned. Sliding the steel pipe from his belt, he got into position in an alcove to the right of the dummy. And there he waited. Earnest got closer and closer, the rifle still locked in his grasp. Then he drifted past with his back to Brody.

He clobbered Earnest in the head. Earnest tumbled forward, hit the support post, and landed on the ground. As he swiftly lifted the pipe to finish the job, Bertram hollered for his brother and an arrow narrowly missed Brody's head.

Pipe in hand, he ducked and charged across the open space like a bull. Catching Bertram in the chest like a quarterback, the older twin lost his footing. They knocked over a replica of an iron maiden. Bertram's recurve cracked, and he groaned and reached for Brody's wounded arm. But Brody punched him in the face and slammed the pipe lengthwise into his throat. Choking, Bertram grabbed the pipe, pushing up. Brody pressed down with his full weight. Writhing beneath him, Bertram spat and gasped and locked his legs around his waist. Brody grimaced as the guy's muscular thighs squeezed. As he struggled for leverage, he sensed someone behind him, and just as he turned to look, the butt of a rifle hit his jaw.

Fuck. I should've shot them both.

~

I WAITED at the side of the haunted house, debating whether I should go in. It was last place I had to search. My heart lurched. There were voices—the voices of two men coming from the inside the building. Lifting the baseball bat, I nervously crept closer to the entrance. The doors opened, and I watched as a pair of identical men in military fatigues dragged Brody by his ankles over the dry, lumpy ground. The whole scene was straight out of a movie. Apparently knocked unconscious, Brody's arms trailed behind him.

"I thought he'd killed you," one man said.

"Me too at first," said the other. He held the back of his skull. "My head really hurts. He got me good."

"Doctor Günter will examine you soon as we finish this."

"He wasn't as tough as I thought he'd be."

I didn't think. I just rushed them, yelling like a madman, and swung. And I was surprised when the baseball bat actually made contact with the injured guy's head. He dropped like a ton of bricks. I stumbled past him, swinging again.

"My brother, you scrawny fuck!" the other man shouted, and I came face-to-face with an arrow and his enraged scowl. But someone grabbed my calf, yanked hard, and just as I fell, the sound of a gunshot echoed off the haunted house and surrounding buildings. Everything happened so fast I didn't have time to comprehend it. I was lying on top of Brody, and I saw the guy with the bow fall over, a bullet lodged in his forehead. Blood streamed his shocked expression, and I looked away.

"Why are you here?" Brody asked.

"I woke up and you were gone. I was worried." I got up and off him, brushing dirt from my hands and pant legs.

He sighed and searched my eyes. "Thank you for the assistance. But I want you to return to the house."

"What? But you're hurt." As he got to his feet and holstered the Beretta, I motioned to the guy I'd knocked out. "There's only him left anyway. You can just kill him, and then we can get out of here."

"Earnest."

"So the dead one is Bertram."

"Yes." He hovered over Earnest, scrutinizing his injury. "The situation isn't as it appears. We must leave."

"I can't believe it. You actually left me behind," I said with exasperation, furiously rubbing my scalp. "God, you know I get it —the whole not wanting to relive what happened with Cody—but I'm not him. I'm different, damn it!" I paused to look him in the face. "I survived Maxine and Jack. Do you know why?"

"Enlighten me," he said, handing me the baseball bat.

"Because of you. Whether you're dying or not, you always come for me. And if the time ever comes when you don't, I'll either find my balls and do something daring, or I won't."

He burst with laughter, a weird and wonderful new facet to his personality, which never ceased to catch me off-guard; he was changing. "You are correct, and I was wrong."

I frowned, pressing the back of my hand to his forehead. "Are you feeling all right?"

He grabbed my nape, leaned close, and kissed me passionately. Then he walked away leaving me dazed and lovestruck. "We need to leave," he added sternly.

"Okay." I came back to my senses. "But what about Earnest?"

"He's irrelevant."

It was strange for Brody to leave an opponent alive, and stranger still that he seemed on edge. I took a last brief look at the unconscious man then followed Brody through the park.

We entered a narrow alley between a row of game shacks and an extended beer garden cordoned off with rope. Brody put a hand to my chest. I stopped and didn't make a sound. The wind picked up speed, and the canvas fringe of the tent roof flapped like a wet sheet pinned to a clothesline. Even with the music and movement of machinery, there was an eerie calm about the place.

Something whizzed through the air and walloped him dead center in the chest. The dart was huge. Scowling, he quickly tore it out and fired into the distance. But no one was there. He blinked and lost his footing. I quickly discarded the baseball bat and steadied him. Then he was hit twice more. Thump, thump, two direct hits from a hard object. The ammunition syringes looked like something used in big game hunting. Freaked, I yanked both out of his back.

He pinched his eyes and faltered a few feet, pushing me out of the way. "Get out of here," he slurred.

Obviously the tranquilizers were fast acting.

"But—"

"Now!"

He never raised his voice, and it got me scared. Unwillingly, I turned back in the direction we'd come from. As I glanced over my shoulder, Brody staggered, the M9 dangling from his fingers, and he collapsed altogether. I broke into a sprint, through the alley and around the bend toward the haunted house. Someone tackled me; we fought. But the man clamped my nose and mouth and shoved a pair of metallic prongs into my ribs. In front of me were several black sedans, at least a dozen heavily-armed men dressed like military police, and an older, bearded man in a brown suit. Anxious, I sucked in a sweaty, dirty smell, yelling and clawing at my subduer. Then electricity fried me from the inside out, until my eyelids felt like lead and everything began to fade. The last thing I saw between flickering lids was the bearded man looking down at me. "Welcome to End Life, Zeus. I hope you enjoy your stay."

AUTHOR'S NOTE

This series has been a blast to write. I wanted to create a dark storyline without boundaries and characters with intrinsic chemistry, which I think worked out pretty well. *Embrace the Reaper* is the final book, and it contains the most emotion. Zeus and Brody have come a long way from their initial encounter. As they confront their most formidable opponent, Zeus finally matures, and Brody seems practically human. If only for a moment, the pair swap identities and get a chance to truly understand one another. Value isn't in the material but in those we hold dear, and love is what makes that value real.

And I looked, and behold, a pale horse: and his name that sate on
him was Death, and hell followed with him.
    — Revelation 6:8

The Holy Bible
    King James Version
    Authorized Version Published 1611

CHAPTER ONE

I dashed into the woods. Every muscle was on fire, and my throat was dry and sore. After running over a mile bathed in moonlight, I lost my bearings in the pitch black. Branches whipped my chest like jellyfish tentacles; one stung under my right eye, splitting the delicate layer of flesh. *Fuck!* I shielded my face, crossing my arms.

The agents' voices and the barking of their tracker dogs were clear and growing louder. And when I peered back, a dozen flashlights floated between the trees like orbs...

~

THE BEGINNING of my end and Brody's started at the Golden Valley Amusement Park. The last thing I remembered was a brief scuffle when someone clamped my mouth and nose, and 50,000 volts surged through my chest, prickling my breath. When I came to, I had a splitting headache. I was strapped to a bed—by my limbs and even my head—and dressed in what looked like plain white pajamas. I saw stark walls and a metal door with a mesh window, like a psychiatric ward. And I knew I was in the End Life facility.

I freaked, screaming and straining against the straps. Seconds in, three men wearing mint-green, straight-cut slacks and smocks entered the room. While two restrained me, the third jabbed me with a needle. A cold sensation rapidly saturated my entire arm then leaked into my chest muscles, freezing me slowly, taking over inch by inch. My heart rate decelerated dramatically, and my head became too heavy for my neck to support. I felt sluggish, worn-out, and vulnerable.

My captors unclasped the leather straps, hoisted me to standing, and stripped me naked. Completely stoned, I possessed no mobility control and fell forward. They hauled me, feet slapping the cool linoleum, through a too-bright corridor. Squinting, I listened to my hollow inhalations. I was a prisoner in my own head. Even if I'd wanted to fight, my body wasn't capable.

The next room was just as bleak as the first, with a solitary, caged light in the ceiling and an execution-style chair in the center. A variety of syringes lined a table against the rear wall, and there was a metal pail on the floor. The men bound my wrists and fore-arms, ankles and calves, to the chair. The bare wood slats pinched my scrotum, and I winced. Worse, I knew they hadn't brought me here to discuss the latest political election.

Once I was secured, the three men in identical uniforms filed out of the room as another man dressed in a white lab coat entered. Middle-aged, tall, broad-shouldered, and towheaded, the man had a goatee and a handsome, leonine profile. He moved with an air of superiority, and his piercing, pale blue gaze never strayed. He was the same man who had spoken to me at the amusement park, just before I was Tasered.

I watched through a murky fog as he picked up the pail and threw the contents at me. Freezing water splashed my face and torso. The cold gave me a jolt. More lucid than I had been seconds earlier, I hung my head, gasping and shivering, as ice cubes settled in my groin and twirled across the floor like translucent ballerinas.

"Where's Brody?" I hissed, spreading my thighs so the ice would slip away.

"Brody is just fine," he replied. "Did you think we'd dispose of our greatest asset? He is worth ten times more than any of the others. He was exceptional from the moment of discovery."

Teeth chattering, I eyed the man; I recognized his German accent. He was the same man Brody had talked to over the phone the night of Maxine's death. "What do you want with me? And why am I naked?"

"We're going to run some tests." He reached back and grasped a syringe filled with clear liquid off the table. "Bare flesh has a way of humbling the subject."

"Is this how you treated Brody, asshole?"

He paused to smile. It was nefarious at best, and I knew I was dealing with a very deranged but intellectually sound man. "Brody's brain works the same as a computer, albeit more advanced. Through simple observation, he can evaluate the emotions and thought patterns of those around him and account for any unpredictable factors, such as a knee-jerk reaction, and more predictable ones such as general behavioral traits shared by all humans. In other words, he has extraordinary insight, and he can turn a wrong situation into a win-win. Whatever scenario he creates in his mind *will come to pass*." He emphasized his words. "He just makes it happen."

Günter paused, his face solemn, then he said in monotone, "For example, we tested him in public once. The subject was a pedophile who had just been released after serving an eighteen-month prison sentence. Under close supervision of one our female staff, a girl, aged six, was placed in a park where other children were playing. She had the physical features the pedophile would find most appealing—golden brown hair and big brown eyes—and she appeared doll-like in her frilly pink dress. We'd been watching the man's movements for weeks, and just as I'd predicted, he returned to the park that day and took notice of the girl."

"Holy shit. You actually used that little girl as bait."

"I did." He folded his arms over his midsection. "Do let me finish. Brody was there as well, of course. We'd allowed him, with no prior information, an hour to observe the playground and assess whatever the situation might be. It was quite remarkable, really, how quickly he pegged the pedophile and his target. Within less than five minutes, he knew why he'd been summoned to the park, and he'd come to the only conclusion he could."

"He killed the man," I said.

Günter's thin-lipped smile was nauseating. "Dennis O'Connor, with the adeptness of a pro, stealthily snatched the girl right from under our female staff member's eyes by giving her a lollipop. He took her by the hand and simply walked away. What he didn't realize was that Brody was lying in wait. So, by the time Dennis reached his minivan, it was already too late. My sweet, *sweet* Brody follows his own code of justice, and anyone he deems detrimental to society is exterminated."

He chuckled, and then said with unbridled delight, "As soon as Dennis opened the side door of the van, Brody grabbed him, dragged him kicking and screaming into the darkness behind the seats, shut the door, and slit him from stem to stern. After which he quickly changed his shirt, removed his gloves, put the soiled clothes and knife in a bag, and then climbed out the rear."

"What about the little girl?"

"Brody walked her back to the park to meet with our female staff member. It was an incredibly touching moment. The child was holding his hand with both of hers, snuggling into his side, scared to let him go. Ah, but what a befitting death!" Günter resumed his position, standing tall in front of me.

"You've been using his ability to control him and make him kill whoever you think should die."

He clasped his hands behind his back, bent forward, and searched my eyes. "I'd assumed you were dull-witted, but that isn't the case. Perhaps you could be reprogrammed."

"You like to toy with peoples' lives. It seems you've got a God complex." I scowled. "Which makes you a coward."

The bastard seized my arm, and the needle sunk into my flesh. In less than a minute, tears were streaming my cheeks as indescribable pain welled up inside me like a geyser, threatening to tear my whole body apart at the seams. I bit my lip. My stomach and abdomen hurt the most, and I groaned, trying to curl in a ball.

"This next injection," he said as he held up a different syringe, "will induce a fight-or-flight response. I can hardly wait to see what you do."

As soon as the narcotic hit my bloodstream, a sense of anxiety came on overpoweringly fast, the likes of which I'd never experienced. My heart pounded, causing my body to tremble and grow clammy, and sweat broke out in beads across my brow. My chest tightened, and I dug my fingers into the armrests, my breathing dipping dangerously to shallow.

Günter untied me, then stood back like an enthusiastic father waiting for his toddler to take its first unaided step. I got up from the chair and managed to stand. I didn't care about him. My only goal was the open doorway. I wandered slowly from the room and fell, my damp back crashing against a corridor wall. Sliding my shoulder along the white paint, I focused on my next goal.

There was an exit just ahead, and I stumbled into it with my arms outstretched. I pushed down on the metal bar. It clicked and clanked, but the door wouldn't budge. Now I knew how a mouse felt running through a maze. I was trapped. Driving my fists into it, I yelled until my voice turned hoarse and the drug wore off, depleted by fatigue and the sense of urgency I felt. I needed to find a toilet before my bodily functions let go. I desperately banged on several doors, rattled the knobs of others, but found neither an escape route nor a washroom. Of course, the inevitable happened.

The men dressed in mint-green returned and walked me, thighs streaked with urine and excrement, to a spacious changing room that had benches, lockers, toilets, and sinks. One of them handed me a bar of soap and pointed to the communal shower.

Grumbling, I snatched the soap. There were no taps. Once I

stood under the showerhead, water rained down at a comfortable temperature.

"You lasted longer than I expected." Günter walked into the room, hands clasped behind his back. "The effects of the drug are short-lived, but I thought the large dose might send you into cardiac arrest."

Sadistic prick. I continued to lather my chest. "Lucky me."

"Yes, lucky you," he said. "Perhaps you will be of some use."

"Where's Brody?"

"He's in his private quarters."

"When can I see him?" I washed my face, allowing the cascade to rinse my torso.

"This isn't summer camp, Zeus. I've separated you for a reason."

I could only begin to surmise what he wanted from me. The real prize was Brody—not some uneducated ex-whore with no skills who lacked a homicidal maniac's mindset. Doctor Günter was just playing with me. For whatever reason, I amused him, and when he grew bored, he'd probably kill me.

After my shower, I was given clothes, fed, and locked in a room with a bed, where I remained.

CHAPTER TWO

I had no contact with the outside world. I never saw any daylight or the moon, and with the continuous adminis- tration of narcotics, the hours—possibly days—ran together until time didn't exist. I was stuck inside a bubble, scarcely able to sleep and fed only the bare minimum required to sustain life. Between short intervals of rest, I was moved from room to room all over the facility, where I endured different physical and mental tests. Most were torturous, and it took all my strength to stay focused. I was scared that if I didn't concentrate, I'd eventually lose my mind, lose myself to the depravity.

Finally, after God knows how many days, I was given a change of clothes and left to rest. But not long into my sleep, I heard a commotion—the hard footfalls of multiple people running in the corridor. I wearily peered over my shoulder. Shadows moved under the bottom of the door. I quickly sat up on my elbows, my heart thudding when a faint cry of agony reached my ears. There was a loud crash and shouting, and then an alarm blared. Sinking back into the bed, I clutched the thin flannel blanket.

Whatever was going on continued for hours.

Then it was mortuary quiet as if nothing had happened, and I slowly drifted to sleep.

Sometime later, one of the men responsible for escorting me from one chamber of horrors to the next held the door open and signaled with a nod. I hesitated before sliding off the bed.

He walked me barefoot through the corridor into an adjacent room, this one the largest I'd seen yet. The white starched walls and ceiling were like a painter's canvas, spotless. Brody was seated erect in a heavy wood chair, the same type they'd strapped me to the day of my arrival.

"Brody!" My anticipation rose with the excitement of a blind date or a first kiss, like when we'd first met. But he didn't blink, and he didn't move. He didn't show any kind of physical response. His eyes were glazed and vacant, with a familiar, eerily lifeless look, only a hundred times worse. Back when Brody had first become my john, and I'd wanted to know more about him, I'd followed him one night into a dance club where a man had just been murdered. When I caught up to Brody outside the club, I saw the soullessness in his eyes. That incident seemed to bind us somehow, and we grew closer, and gradually he changed. But now, the Brody I'd known and loved wasn't in the room. There was only one plausible reason why he wouldn't respond: he'd forgotten me. "Please," I begged softly, touching his chin. "Please remember me."

"The chances of that are slim to none."

I looked behind to see Doctor Günter in the doorway, his ghostly hair slicked back and his hands tucked inside the oversized square front pockets of his lab coat. "What have you done to him?"

"He's been given a mild sedative." Günter shut the door and slid the heavy deadbolt into place.

"Why?"

"Because he's unpredictable."

I didn't know much about mental disorders or even if my lover suffered from one, but the sedative seemed to be doing more than keeping him calm. Brody appeared to be in a catatonic state, unreachable, and that fucking terrified me. "So you *are* scared of the Reaper."

"The Reaper... I chose that nickname to incite fear in his victims," he said acridly, tapping his own chest. "I wanted him to become a legend, like King Arthur—regarded as historical fact but never authenticated, as infamous as he was powerful."

King Arthur? This guy was a nut—king of the nuts. I kept close to Brody, hoping that he'd wake and end our incarceration.

"It took years to mold him. Now it's in danger of unraveling, thanks to you. I'm concerned with his behavior."

"Yeah, I suppose it does pose a problem when the lunatics start running the asylum." I laughed despite how absolutely furious I was.

"Your humor is tasteless."

"And you're a megalomaniac." I glared every inch of the man down. "This isn't a Mary Shelley novel, and you sure as *hell* aren't Doctor Frankenstein—at least he cared about his creation!"

He eyed me grimly, walking toward us; I'd deflated just a bit of his God complex. "You can read."

I shrugged, the sarcasm rolling off my tongue. "I get by."

"People demand justice, and Brody here"—he clamped Brody's shoulder—"gives them all the justice they can handle. He's the archetype for my Snuff program, but, sadly, he's a failure. However, if he kills you, he'll be deemed a success. Then his memories will be purged, and he'll be relocated to start a new objective."

"What the fuck does that mean?"

"I suppose it's only fair to explain since you're not leaving here alive."

His condescending attitude made me clench my teeth.

"To clarify: Brody has feelings for you. Unfortunately, that is one thing End Life hasn't been able to nullify. The frontal lobe controls essential cognitive skills. It's the moral compass and motherboard of the human personality, and to maintain control, that section of the brain cannot be tampered with in any way. We injected drugs to inhibit suggestion. Everything Brody has become is the result of years of psychological manipulation and indoctrination. Otherwise, he'd just kill and spare at will—inefficient behavior for a killing machine. But at the same time, he has to retain some empathy to focus."

"Then the last two years have been a trial run?"

"That's correct. He was ordered to kill only those people whom society sees as disposable: johns and pimps."

I thought about Gino and the men who had beaten and raped me. If it weren't for Brody, I would've eventually taken my own life. He'd saved me from a very dark place, something the callous, egotistical man in front of me could not conceive. I knew Brody better than anyone. Even if he'd been conditioned to become a psychotic killer, he'd never harm me.

"Anyway, none of that matters now." Günter knocked on the door. "Today, everything changes."

The door opened and four burly men, each armed with a pistol, entered the room. Sensing that the situation was about to go from bad to worse, I instinctively backed away from Brody. As I did, the men took positions behind him in a crescent.

Günter leaned over Brody. "I know you're a good boy," he cooed softly in his ear, staring straight at me while loosening the straps. "If you kill the whore, I'll forget the past two years, and you'll be permitted to select the targets you like. Fail here...and Earnest will find him. You've got one bullet, so make it count."

Brody blinked slowly as Günter wrapped his awakening fingers around his favorite weapon, a Beretta. The men aimed at him. Günter took no more interest in me. As he paused at the door, his gaze swept the length of my body from head to toe like I was trash. "We'll see who wins."

"Nobody's going to win here!" I spat as the door clicked shut and the deadbolt locked. *Fucking bastard.* Sucking in a deep breath, I calmed and switched my attention back to the situation at hand. If Brody caught even a whiff of my anxiety, his natural proclivity to murder would put an end to my life. Game or not, I had to prove to the crazy psychiatric scientist that I didn't fear my lover but trusted him implicitly. The old man had demanded Brody kill me to prove his loyalty, prove that he hadn't gone rogue.

Brody lifted the gun.

"I love you," I declared, closing my eyes, hoping my death would be instantaneous.

One.

Two.

Each second was excruciating.

There was a very loud bang followed by a commotion and additional gunfire. I flinched.

Then deafening silence.

When I opened my eyes, Brody was panting in front of me, a different gun at his side. The men lay dead on the floor. I didn't dare move, and I saw a painful reality in his eyes; no longer stoic, he looked on the verge of tears. "Thank you for trusting me," he said. "I know it's difficult, but I need you to continue to trust me."

Surprised, I could only nod.

"Günter will return in a moment, so listen carefully."

"Yes."

"Whatever he tells you to do, I want you to agree. However, I don't want you to follow through with his instructions. Instead, I want you to get as far from here as possible. Remember: show no fear."

"*Show no fear*," I mimicked like a parrot.

"Do you understand?"

"Yes. But what about you?"

"Don't worry, I'll find you."

He flashed a grin, but it was artificial, a ruse to hide the truth, his concerns, and, once again, I felt helplessly sick to my stomach. But before I could speak, Günter had slipped back inside the room.

The psychiatrist took one look at the bloody scene. "You're such a disappointment." He snatched the gun from Brody, who remained stationary like a mannequin. "I gave you one command!"

Brody didn't answer and continued to stare vacantly past me; the second his teacher had reappeared, he shut down.

"Do you love him?" Günter asked me.

I was startled by the question but answered honestly. "Yeah."

His voice penetrated like a shard of ice as he placed a new semi-automatic pistol on the table. *Talk about a one-track mind.* "Then I'll make a deal with you, Zeus."

"What kind of deal?" I was willing to do just about anything to get us out of the funny farm, and I'd agreed to Brody's terms.

"Earnest is roaming free somewhere in the lower levels of this facility. That's why this floor is on lockdown. If you kill him, I'll release you both."

I peered through my stringy bangs. The guy deserved a bullet between the eyes, but I didn't have fast enough reflexes to shoot him, nor was my aim accurate. "You really get off on this shit, don't you?"

Doctor Günter smirked, his lip line razor-sharp, in a look so familiar I got the chills. Like mentor like student. Brody's eyes were lifeless once again. I had no idea if he was even in the room with us. After having his brain psychologically sliced and diced, there was no guarantee he'd ever be one hundred percent the same. But I just couldn't give up. The memories were still so fresh in my mind, from the day we'd first met to the last time we'd made love. Fighting back the tears, I made my demands, showing zero fear as Brody had instructed. "Fine, I'll do it," I said. "But you and End Life can never come after us again. Once Earnest is dead, it's over, and we walk out of here alive together."

"Agreed."

Glaring at the doctor, I brushed past, swiping the pistol from the table.

～

FROM THE FOREST, I flew into a glade, but I only got a few yards before Earnest walloped me in the gut. I stopped dead, clutching my midsection. He punched me in the face. I fell backward to land hard on my tailbone and cried out as the shock rattled my spine. Then I scrambled to crawl away, but he grabbed my hair and yanked me sideways. Knees scraping through the dirt and gravel, I hollered, fighting to loosen his grip. I remembered the gun Günter had given me.

"You dumb fuck!" he spat and punched me again. "I'll kill you!"

Blinded by stars, I faltered like a puppet on a string and quickly wound up back on all fours. I stared wearily at the lumpy grass, disoriented, wondering where I'd lost the gun. Then his boot came into contact with my abdomen. Intense pain hitched my breath, and I retched violently. Blood mixed with mucus covered my hand in a slimy film as I shakily wiped my mouth.

"Hey!" a man shouted.

Earnest ducked, edging away, and darted into the woods. Lying on my back, panting, I heard more voices and the rustle of grass. When I moved, my arm brushed a hard object: the Beretta. The End Life agents had nearly caught up with me. I'd escaped the main perimeter, and the alarms were blaring. The agents had to get us back inside before the local authorities were notified. I got onto my hands and knees, rose with one hand on my stomach, and limped heavily in the same direction Earnest had taken.

I had no idea where to go but assumed that the psycho did, so I followed his trail of broken branches and flattened underbrush. He had lived in the pharmaceutical company's housing units for over a year, according to conversations I'd overheard between different members of staff, so he knew the layout of the entire facility. And I didn't want the agents to catch me because I'd get a Taser to the ribs and end up in solitary again. Just the thought of more drug-induced experiments made me break out in a cold sweat.

CHAPTER THREE

"*W*hat a brave soul. Earnest will rip him to shreds." Günter stood in the middle of the blood, a dealer of antiquities admiring his collection of priceless objects. "See, I told you. You have no qualms when it comes to facing any threat." He pointed an accusatory finger at Brody. "That whore owns you."

Brody slowly lifted his gaze.

"Don't bother denying it. What happened to that fire inside of you? It used to burn so brightly. It's as if you're a different person. Distant." Günter sighed, slapping his palms on the tabletop. "Keep ignoring me, and I'll castrate him, so he'll never experience another orgasm again."

"What would you have me say?" Brody asked evenly, clenching his jaw.

"I want you to obey only me!"

He turned to the older man. "Release him, and I promise to stay."

"What do you take me for? I know you'd do anything for him. It's apparent by your actions that you feel for him."

"I'm incapable."

"No. You're not." Günter shook his head. "I never thought

you'd betray me," he said bitterly. "But that whore has awakened something in you...something I never could."

"Please, David, release me."

"Earnest is frothing at the mouth. All you did was antagonize him. You should've killed him when you had the opportunity."

"Zeus comes first. I had to protect him."

"God, it's sickening how you go on and on about him. You're obsessed."

Brody watched Günter pace the room with hands loosely clasped at his lower back, and his own thoughts were tugged away by the darkness. He'd told Zeus once: *Needs must when the devil drives.* He knew the only way to get out of the room was to verbally prostrate himself. So he set aside the one sentiment that fueled his wrath. Brusquely, he approached the older man, grasped either side of his face, and searched his pale irises, easing into a kiss. "I promise I will make you my bitch. However, I must kill them first. A clean slate. It's the only way."

Günter stared at his mouth, acknowledging the affection with a grunt.

Brody reached behind the man's back, confiscating the gun. "Tell me to do it," he goaded quietly against his lips. "Tell me to fuck them up."

"God, do you know how hard I am right now?"

It was simple to detect Günter's excitement. All he had to do was get close enough, allow his senses to absorb the data, then his computer like brain would analyze it: raspy, agitated breathing, dilated pupils, skin radiating pheromone infused heat, and a rosy complexion. The doctor was a sexually frustrated mess. If it were Zeus panting and all feverish, Brody would have fucked him right there on the table. But the older man did nothing to rouse his libido.

"I know." He breathed hot on the doctor's Adam's apple, and Günter swallowed. Then he took the torment a bit further. He spread the doctor's thighs with his knee, nudging his swollen crotch, and the man landed on the edge of the table, sliding the piece of furniture with his weight.

"Don't tease," Günter groaned, eyelids fluttering.

"Say it."

"F-Fuck them up," Günter urged with the eagerness of a child.

Sliding the bullet chamber, Brody let him go and grinned. "Everyone will die."

"So long as it's you, my sweet, I don't care."

Brody exited the room to the blare of the central alarm, frantic shouts from staff members, doors slamming, and the tremor of movement as guards approached a pair of men who were stabbing each other. He turned west and stepped around a dead woman on the way to the communal showers, where orderlies struggled to subdue a male in his late teens. As he passed the commotion, his eyes locked with the teenager's, and he knew the kid was an inductee—glazed, lifeless pupils were a definite sign of Doctor Günter's methods of proselytization. But as the four crashed into the doors, he noticed something else. The kid was holding a steel pipe pitted with rust.

He immediately changed his course, entered the concrete room, shot each orderly dead, then aimed at the teen, who hastily crab-walked back into a row of lockers.

"I know who you are." The kid stared blankly.

"Give it to me."

"This?" The kid looked at the pipe in surprise. "What's a gunslinger like you want with a dinky piece of metal?"

"I prefer well-used things."

"You really wanna sock it to someone."

"I enjoy the sound a bone makes when it breaks." Brody frowned and pointed the gun at the kid's forehead. "But I also enjoy watching the trail of carnage a bullet leaves behind as it burrows through human flesh."

The kid laughed nervously, tossing the pipe on the tile floor with a loud clank that echoed off the brick tomb. "Take it. It's yours."

"A wise decision." Brody was scooping up the pipe and heading for the door when he heard a click. Whipping his arm back, he fired, and a bullet drilled the teen's chest dead center. The kid gulped, wide-eyed, shakily setting a revolver on the floor. "However, that decision was not," Brody said gravely, as the boy breathed his last. He'd taken no enjoyment in killing him. Perhaps he was losing his taste for it because the only objective he had in mind was to save Zeus. Zeus had become his reason for living—and his pretext to eliminate anyone who stood in his way.

Discarding the gun, he strode out of the communal shower with his newly acquired weapon. No one was in sight. At the end of the wide corridor, he pushed on the exterior exit door and walked into the glow of silvery moonlight and the stale humidity of a muggy summer evening. The alarm wasn't so deafening outside. He noted several black lumps—bodies lying in the grass—before a gunshot, and the barking of dogs in the distance caught his attention. Studying the forested area, he allowed the pipe to slip a bit lower before retightening his grip. There were four directions he could take, and he chose north. His instinct told him it was the correct path, and he took off running, to be swallowed by the murky woods.

He saw every living thing, frame by frame: the pine needle-littered forest floor, rocks, the gnarled roots of trees, ferns, toadstools, and the white luminosity of tiny, bell-shaped white flowers that perfumed the air with an intoxicating scent. In all the years he'd spent in captivity, he'd never bothered to appreciate his surroundings. But now he noticed the beauty; he was drenched in it. Zeus needed to see the forest. And he wanted to show him. *Maybe there's hope for my wretched soul yet.* He smirked and sped up.

Soon the trees thinned, and he came face-to-face with a new challenger. The blond was one of Günter's personal guards, of German descent, tall and ripped. His body language made it clear he wasn't about to back down.

"We can either do this the easy way or..." Adalard pitted his fist into his palm and flexed his biceps.

Brody stood with his legs slightly apart, pipe still in hand. He studied his opponent, wondering if everything he'd gone through had come down to this moment. Adalard was a fighter, ex-military, probably one of the best he'd encountered during his instruction in the Snuff program—at the least, the most proficient out of all the trainers and the closest to Brody's physical equal.

"Where's Zeus?"

"Dead, I hope. That guy's more trouble than he's worth."

Dead, I hope. The statement stung. As he considered his current state of affairs with more care, every memory of Zeus over the past two years surfaced. He stared vacantly. *How could I be so obtuse?*

"Took you long enough," Adalard said, adopting a combative stance.

"I've been duped."

"Doctor Günter wanted you to become emotionally attached."

"An experiment."

"He said that given a 'precise set of circumstances,' you'd eventually kill the slut and revert back to your true nature."

"That will never happen."

"Yes, that's why we're here." Adalard reached behind his back. "When he realized you'd actually fallen in love, he said you had to die."

The truth was ugly, as was Brody's denial of it. His life had been forfeit to Günter from the very beginning—the most manipulative serial killer of all had seduced and used him. The burn crawled up from the base of Brody's skull, and his skin tingled; he almost yelled. Due to the folly of his actions, he'd been played like a fiddle, and Zeus's life had been put in jeopardy. He tried to remain calm, to rationally consider every angle. Closing his eyes, he exhaled extra slowly and focused on Adalard, blocking all other stimuli from his mind. "Do you remember my training?"

"You were a feisty bastard who rarely followed the rules."

"I should've killed you then."

"I'm guessing you don't like me."

"Apparently."

"Well." The guard laughed, goading Brody with a flick of his hands. "Now's your chance, *Mr. Reaper*."

"An oversight on my part." He squeezed the pipe, the pits of rust sharp as slivers of glass. "I won't make the same mistake twice."

"I'm going to fucking enjoy this!" Adalard lunged, swinging, his cold eyes brimming with crazed lust.

Brody dodged the twelve-inch military-issue blade and swung. The pipe cracked Adalard in the ribs. He groaned, holding his side, stumbling a few feet away, but immediately countered, taking another swipe. Brody tilted his head back as the knife nicked his throat. He felt the pinch and flow of blood. And he brought the pipe down hard on the guy's forearm. Adalard cried out, letting go of his weapon, and Brody went ballistic. He timed every strike perfectly with his breathing. The trainer's flesh broke, as did his cartilage and bones. Soon, the man was lying unconscious on the ground, a bloody pulp.

Licking his lips, Brody took a step back, the blood warm on his face and hands.

"Brody!"

He honed in on his lover's voice as he limped into the clearing. "Zeus..." He started to walk toward him but frowned as a dark figured moved in behind.

CHAPTER FOUR

"Watch out!" Brody's voice echoed off the wall of sardine-packed trees.

I spun around. Earnest jabbed at me. I recoiled, bending my torso into a crescent as Brody's pipe made contact with the guy's jaw. It happened in jumpy, slow motion, a snippet of film out of sync as I fell. Then the momentum returned to normal, and Brody was swinging like a major league batter. His dead gaze was transfixed as he sent Earnest careening into the tall grass.

But the bastard was quick to recover. He leaped to his feet and came at Brody. Tackled at the waist, Brody lost the pipe and was driven to the ground. He gasped, struggling, as they tussled about, and eventually Earnest got the upper hand. He punched Brody over and over. With a busted lip and bleeding nose, Brody fought back, and they rolled around like snakes in a pit, each vying for control.

Earnest lifted his leg and straddled Brody's midsection, yelling and stabbing viciously in downward thrusts. His frenzied attack almost caused my heart to stop. Brody blocked the large knife with crossed arms. Dread seized my entire being, choking me. Blood—

Brody's blood—was everywhere as the sharp steel nicked him here and there.

I limped nearer, held the gun with both my hands, raised it, and squeezed the trigger. "No!"

The bullet missed.

Fuck!

Earnest looked my direction, snarled like a crazed beast, and sprang into the air.

Fuck!

I stopped short and took aim. Quivering, I fired a second shot. The bullet tore his shoulder, blasting tissue and fragments of bone into the atmosphere, but it did little to deter the homicidal maniac. Hollering, he lunged for me, but as he did Brody pounced on him and grappled his head, forcing it back before driving the pipe into the guy's throat and yanking it out. Blood spilled, a waterfall soaking Earnest's shirt. Eyes saucer-wide, Earnest dropped the knife and reached, clawing at Brody. I remained motionless, entranced by the violence. Then it was over. Earnest gradually sagged to the ground as a pool leaked from under his cheek, the parched grass drinking it in.

I jumped at the loud reverberation of a gunshot.

Deep lines of pain creased Brody's forehead and the right side of his chest burst. Wet spattered my face. I cringed. Still holding the pipe, he looked me straight in the eyes, and for the first time ever a tear escaped from his own. Initially, I was stunned and couldn't react. Then Doctor Günter came into focus directly behind him; the ancient fucker had a Luger.

"Now you'll never have him," he said with a cocksure smile.

In the moments to follow, all the inhibitions that had held me back and kept me morally grounded evaporated. "You fucking bastard!" I roared, squeezing. The gun jerked my wrist, and the last bullet hit its mark. With a hole in his head, Brody's taskmaster hardened like a Greek statue drying in the sweltering heat of a Mediterranean afternoon. God knows how I'd hit him. I'd just aimed and fired. Normally, I didn't have the guts to squash a spider. But right then I'd found my resolve.

Faltering like a drunk, Brody crashed out in the grass to lie beside Earnest. Blood spread, wildfire fast, brilliant red flames devouring his shirt and creeping outwards, marking the bullet's point of exit.

Crumpling to my knees, I put the Beretta down. Brody seemed to look straight through me as if I wasn't there, and sorrow filled his gaze—sorrow stained with regret. He blinked, and tears ran down his cheek. Something told me he wasn't going to make it, and my heart banged. Suddenly, he was flesh and bone—a living and breathing human being that I loved, not the killing machine they'd taught him to be.

"You can't die," I ordered, applying pressure to his wound.

"Death is inevitable for me," he wheezed, "but not for you."

I cinched his shirt and yanked him close. Sniveling, I bit back my breath, resting my forehead on his collarbones. "No. You have to live. You *must* live."

"The government is involved now. The police will come."

"I'm not leaving you behind!" I was incensed that he refused to listen to reason, refused to be with me, refused to live. Something had to be done. I couldn't just leave him to die. "Besides," I said as I wrapped his arm around my neck and braced his back, "you're tough, the toughest person I know. You're going to survive this."

I strained to lift him. "Please, baby, work with me." He finally complied, slowly getting to his feet with my assistance. But I knew he wasn't doing it to save himself. He was doing it to satisfy my wishes.

"That's good. Come on." Holding his waist snugly, I helped him cross the rear grounds of the facility. We entered the central building via an emergency exit. The alarm was still blaring as we shuffled through the now-empty corridor.

I checked each room as we went until I found what appeared to be the infirmary. Brody groaned under his breath as he eased back onto the gurney. His clammy flesh was pale. I shoved a pillow under his head and stuffed the wound with yards of gauze; then I placed his hand on top. I had to find help, and quickly.

"I'll be right back, okay?"

"Where are you going?" He clamped my wrist with an iron grip, his watery gaze fixed on me.

"To find help, of course."

"No one will help me."

"They will."

"I told you, Zeus. You must leave."

My chest sank and I could hardly gulp down the knot in my throat. I lost my temper. "I love you so much, you selfish prick!"

CHAPTER FIVE

*B*rody wanted to say, 'I love you too,' but sharing his thoughts in that instant would've been cruel, detrimental. Zeus needed a clean break. Any emotional outpouring could get him killed. Besides, such desires were immaterial now. "I know you do. Go."

"I don't care if I die. I want to be with you forever."

"Defiant as always." Brody sighed, then said with genuine feeling, "However, I do care. Now please leave."

He was surprised but overwhelmed when the once shy and introverted young ex-prostitute kissed him passionately before releasing his hand. Zeus wiped his face, his effort wasted as more tears trickled down his cheeks. His blood-stained mouth and chin quivered as he unsteadily backed away.

Brody listened as Zeus ran from the room, sneakers squeaking on the polished cement. Then he rolled his head to the side, and the wide, rectangular window greeted him with a perfect view. The sky was turbulent: creamy gray and white clouds amalgamating with brilliant blue as the dawn's first light tried to wake the earth. After a period, he heard more footsteps, but these were distinctive —light yet determined, drilling into the cement heel to toe.

A woman looked down at him, her chestnut curls dangling over him like upside-down spires ready to strike. She had pretty features, especially her large, dark irises flecked with gold. He wanted to touch her flawless skin, make sure she was real. But he couldn't move his limbs anymore; they hung heavy, like weights on a fishing line. And her white lab coat, pure as a snowflake, came in and out of focus, as if he was adjusting binoculars. *Maybe heaven is white*. He wasn't afraid to die, because death held no meaning. But losing Zeus did. The young man had become his entire world, consumed his every thought, and had somehow salvaged his blackened heart.

Intellectual as he was, he'd found himself influenced by Zeus's generosity and love. He dared to think good thoughts when they were together. The loss of those things, the loss of his humanity, was all that he feared.

So this is love... For over two years his emotions had been staring him in the face. He'd just overanalyzed. But why...when the answer was so simple? He smiled to himself. He was finally free, liberated from a lifetime of self- deprecation.

The woman smoothed his damp hair from his brow, her fingers cool, her actions comforting. "I've only got one question," she said. "Why did you do it?"

It was a logical question. End Life had to be eliminated in order for Zeus to continue living. He grinned and murmured, "Love."

CHAPTER SIX

"Zeus?"

I closed my book and set it in my lap. The man was wearing mirrored sunglasses, a plain black suit and white dress shirt, and he had a strange tattoo on his right hand—a snake with its coils encasing an Irish harp. He had a rough, square jawline wreathed in dark stubble, and a smooth scalp that reflected the sunlight. Built like a small tank, he pulled out a chair and sat at the table, filling the entire breadth of the armrests.

I had a sip of my beer. The weather was gorgeous, so the outdoor terrace of the restaurant was busy. People crowded the tables around us, talking and eating. The umbrella in the stand beside me shifted a little with a tugging gust of warm wind.

"I wished we could've met under better circumstances," he said. "My name is Nicolas Bainbridge, and I'm an attorney for the Aherne family." He removed an envelope from an inside breast pocket, placed the envelope on the table, pressed his fingertips into it, and then slid it over to me. "In the event of his passing, Mr. Aherne instructed me to give you this."

"Mr. Aherne...?"

He leaned close and said discreetly, "Brody, sir."

The moment I heard Brody's name, the anguish I'd suppressed threatened to spill. Rolling my watery eyes, I focused on the bottle and cleared my throat. "Sorry, he never told me his surname. Actually, he never told me much about himself, personal or otherwise... Well that's not entirely true." I expelled an uneasy laugh, giving the back of my head a rub. "I mean, he told me about his relationship with a classmate. And that was kind of personal."

"Don't agonize over it. You are nothing alike."

"You knew him." I dropped my gaze and inhaled a mouthful of beer.

"I met him on occasion. He visited Mr. Aherne's childhood home often."

"Was he nice?"

"Very much so. Incidentally, however, he was also an airhead."

I suddenly giggled again, slamming my bottle on the table; the man had an impeccably polite sense of humor. "Thanks. That makes me feel much better."

"As I said, there is no comparison." He paused. "I will visit you on the first of every month until the estate is gone."

"Every month? But why?"

"Mr. Aherne has left you his entire fortune. Inside the envelope there is five thousand in cash, the key to his parents' house, and a copy of his last will and testament, along with my business card. Should you need my assistance, please don't hesitate to call."

I hastily tore open the envelope, and everything was there just as he'd described. "How much is the estate?"

"Let me put it this way. I'm sure we will become very good friends throughout the remainder of your life."

"This is unreal," I mumbled, examining his hammered features. "I can't possibly accept."

He rose from the table, pushing the chair back. "He loved you, Zeus. No one else has the legal right to claim what belonged to him."

Shortly after my meeting with the attorney, I moved into Brody's family home. And Bainbridge did meet me on the first of every month after that. It didn't take long for me to familiarize myself with the town of Golden Valley. With a minimal population, most of the area was dedicated to farming and sprawling estates.

Before I knew it, a year had passed. Slapping money on the counter at a local pub, I ordered a beer on tap. The bartender thanked me and set a large mug ringed in foam in front of me. I drank and smoked in silence, as I'd done every week since Brody had left me: one drink savored every Friday night. I did it partly to commemorate my loss, but also to keep my memories alive. The pub interior had a muddy, rundown quality, like something out of a gangster movie. There was a handful of locals drinking alone like me. I gulped the last, tangy mouthful, got up, and sauntered toward the entrance. Outside, I shoved my fists inside my jacket pockets.

After Brody died, I contacted one the biggest names in journalism and told him my story and the truth about End Life. The pharmaceutical giant's fall from grace became headline news in every tabloid in the country. Telling the world about Brody and our relationship was the only way to guarantee my safety. As soon as the story broke, a government official came to see me, and subsequent to our meeting, they shut down what remained of End Life and classified all documentation pertaining to the Snuff program as top secret. Public access to the files wasn't permitted. The Feds brought charges against End Life's CEO and members of the board, everything from tax evasion to murder—anything they could use as fodder. And the remaining serial killers, trainees on the list, were shipped to a maximum-security psychiatric hospital. As for me, I watched from the sidelines. Brody's kind would never be used for financial or political gain again.

Television didn't interest me. So, I ate my dinner to voices from the radio in the great room while skimming the pages of a book on Celtic mythology I'd found at the local library. The radio provided comfort, a human voice other than my own. I went through the same routine every night.

After dinner, I trudged the towering curved staircase of polished hardwood. The second floor of the house was opulent with large furnished to excess bedrooms and spa like bathrooms. I didn't occupy the master suite. It seemed inappropriate since I was a stranger living in the home. I used Brody's room instead.

On my way to the bathroom, I stripped. When I got to my jeans, I hopped on one foot then the other, pulling the soft, worn material until my legs were free. I flicked on the lights and fan, leaving my jeans on the carpet and the door partially open. Steam rose like smoke, buffeting the ceiling, as I fiddled with the faucets.

Minutes later, I was rubbing the back of my head dry and wandering into the coolness of the bedroom, when I stopped dead. My jeans were hung neatly on the chair at the desk. A long time ago, I would've panicked, but living alone for so long and after everything that had happened, I'd become wary of my surroundings. I'd traded in ignorance for vigilance, and I had no patience for other peoples' head games. "So, you want to fuck with me, eh?" I muttered, hurriedly dressing and reaching under the pillows on the bed. I'd grown accustomed to carrying a gun. This time it was loaded, and I wasn't scared to use it. Practice made perfect, and I'd spent many nights at the old amusement park, unloading magazines inside the haunted house.

Pistol in hand, I cautiously checked the closet and under the bed, then padded in silence up behind the bedroom door. Peeking into the hallway, I saw no one but edged slowly toward the next bedroom. Once I'd confirmed it was only me on the upper level, I carefully descended the stairs to the lower floor. While nearing the last few steps, I crouched to scan the foyer and wide hallway.

It didn't take me long to discover that absolutely nothing else was out of place. I exhaled. Either the person who'd hung my jeans on the chair had left, or else I had a ghost.

The radio was still on as I leaned against the open refrigerator door, scrutinizing the contents of the shelves. No beer, but there were coolers. I cracked open a can of hard lemonade, took a swig, and shuffled into the great room. I set the gun down, flopped out on the roomy couch, and bunched a cushion under my elbow. And that's when I heard it. Someone or something made a noise, and it wasn't the local news. I nervously peered through the dim lighting, pressing the volume down on the remote.

Movement at the patio slider off the kitchen ignited my fight-or-flight response. I snatched the gun from the coffee table and kept my thumb on the safety. "Who's there?"

A breeze lifted the curtains, and a dark figure emerged amid the flutter of material. I slowly rose from the couch. The Reaper's gray eyes blazed silver in the cast of moonlight. He appeared to be in good physical shape, and he was more handsome than in my memories—he wore no glasses, and his raven-black hair wasn't long but cropped. The man I'd worshiped and the only person I'd ever loved was alive. My mind drew a blank. I was bereft of anything clever to say. The pistol shook in my grasp.

"Doctor Günter's assistant Sheilah performed emergency surgery."

I managed to eke out a whisper. "She saved you..."

"She said I had to prove the world wrong. I still have my doubts that a serial killer can become one hundred percent human."

"What kind of shit are you spewing?" I choked out. My tone was accusing. "Do you have any idea how I feel right now?"

"Infuriated. Hurt."

"I've missed you so much!"

"I needed time to heal. However, when your unabashed account of our relationship made headline news, it forced me to stay in hiding longer than I wanted."

Tears stung my cheeks and ran down to my neck, and I bent an arm over my face. "I'm s-sorry." My heart was pounding, and I couldn't bear to look at him any longer for fear he was a hoax. But when he touched the nape of my neck, I lowered the gun, and it fell from my grasp, hitting the carpet with a thud near my bare feet. The soothing warmth of his lips was on my cheek, and the feeling of his fingers as they sank into my hair was something that had only happened in my dreams. I closed my eyes as he kissed my forehead, my nose, my lips. He was real, and he'd come back to me.

"Love at first sight is still incomprehensible to me. And yet, the moment you entered the lobby at the Regent, I had to have you... I love you, Zeus," he said with feeling, searching my eyes. "I adore you."

"You love me?"

"It is an unhealthy fixation. I am obsessive, controlling, and dangerous."

"Whatever. So am I. As long as we're together, I don't care."

"Maybe there's hope for me yet."

I held his face with both my hands; the man never ceased to take my rationality away. "Never. You're perfect the way you are."

CHAPTER SEVEN

*E*ight years later...

I POURED A CUP OF COFFEE, set the pot back on the percolator, and slouched against the counter, preparing to take a sip. But as I brought the steaming black liquid to my lips, I noticed a box on the kitchen table wrapped in blue and white polka-dot paper and tied with a big, bold, blue bow. Setting the cup down, I opened the tiny card first. I laughed. The message simply read, *Happy B-Day, Baby*. The digital camera inside was exactly what I'd wanted since learning to use our computer. Photography had become a hobby and my saving grace. I had several cameras but not a fully loaded digital that could produce movie-quality footage.

I removed the lens cap and held the camera to my face, squinting to see through the viewfinder. Brody embraced me from behind, and I felt the heat of his breath on my temple. He didn't waste any time and unclasped the buckle at the front of my jeans, unzipping my fly while kissing my nape. "I hope you aren't busy," he whispered.

"Not really. I was just admiring the birthday gift you gave me... Thank you." I glanced back at him, and he grinned, sliding his hand inside my underwear. I moaned, lost my balance, and bent forward, nearly dropping the camera as he fondled my damp cock until it was standing eagerly at attention. His fingers teased, tugging and gently pulling; I couldn't handle anymore. Placing the camera on the kitchen island, I anxiously pushed my jeans and underwear down. The weighty material fell past my knees to land on the tile, bunching around my ankles with a muted clink of the belt buckle. My hard cock sprang free, the glans slick. I tried to kick the jeans away, but Brody stepped on them instead, pinioning my feet as I focused on a droplet of red paint on his runner. He shoved me between the shoulder blades, and I was forced to grasp the counter.

"I'm going to fuck you raw," he said in my ear, and my heart fluttered.

He took the bottle of olive oil from the condiment tray, uncapped the lid, and poured some on my spine. It ran down into the crack of my ass, dripped from my balls, and followed the curve of my inner thighs. I bit my lower lip, clawing at the marbleized granite as he worked it inside my hole with three fingers at once. I'd never been so turned on in my life; I nearly came from the forcefulness of his actions.

"Fuck me," I moaned anxiously, reaching back to spread my ass. "Fuck me now."

He quickly got into position, and his hairy legs brushed mine. He rubbed the swollen head of his cock up and down between my slippery buttocks then plunged inside to the hilt, burning hot and hard as a rock. Grabbing my hips, Brody let off a manly growl, while I exhaled a squeal like a punctured balloon would make.

"Yeah... Agh, that's it," I gasped, my voice faltering the harder he slammed into me, the loud slapping of our flesh filling the kitchen. "There... Fuck me..." Closing my eyes, I stroked my shaft, lustful moans rising from my throat. I was on the verge. *Just a little...* "More, baby," I croaked. Brody thrust deeper, and his long prick nudged the right spot. Suddenly the room exploded in white, a blinding ecstasy. I cried out, jerking myself faster. Brody abruptly hugged my midsection with one arm, and his other held my chest, his fingers on my throat. I rested my head on his shoulder as he groaned hot against my neck. His cock was pulsating inside me with the release of his affection, and my ass twitched. I could scarcely breathe.

"You're beautiful," he whispered breathlessly, kissing me. "I love you."

I don't know why, but my ears burned. I put my hand over my mouth, blushing like a young girl who'd just been kissed for the first time, and I stared through a ridge of moisture at the ceiling.

"Why are you crying?" He kissed my cheek.

"I-I don't know," I sniveled, turning around to face him, as he lifted his foot from my jeans.

"Overwhelmed?"

"Maybe." Sinking into his warm embrace, I hugged him. "Actually, I think it's because you've changed so much."

"You don't care for the new, emotionally attuned me?"

I straightened, looked him in the eyes, and touched his cheek. "Listen carefully. I love the new you *and* the old you. It's just that sometimes your idea of romance catches me off-guard." I wiped olive oil from my backside and wiggled my greasy fingers in his face. "And what the hell is it with the food products lately? First, it was whipped cream, then it was ice cream, and now it's oil. I'm not a Greek salad. There is lube in the house."

"Spontaneity is important in a relationship, as is experimentation." He grinned, cleaning his groin.

"Right." I tore several sheets of paper towel from the rack. "You've been surfing those weird foreign porn websites late at night again."

Pulling up his pants, Brody didn't say a word, but his razor-sharp smile told me I'd hit the nail on the head.

"Spontaneity and experimentation my ass," I grumbled, mopping my crotch.

The doorbell rang, a cascading melody of high and low notes. We both looked at one another, then in the direction of the front foyer.

Brody zipped his fly and dumped the crumpled paper towel in the garbage can under the sink. "I'll answer the door."

"But what if the person recognizes you?"

"No matter what happens, stick to what we've discussed." He walked out of the kitchen, and I flew into action, cleaning myself and getting dressed.

We had a contingency plan in place. We'd set it up years ago just in case someone was to discover that Brody wasn't actually his twin brother Angus. Brody went to great lengths and spent a lot of money to change his identity to that of his dead twin: photos, legal documents, education records, family history, occupational history. After End Life collapsed and everything became public, Brody Aherne could no longer exist; for all intents and purposes, he died that day at the facility along with everyone else. Doctor Günter's assistant Sheilah, who was a surgeon, saved Brody's life and helped him swap identities to escape legal prosecution. She and Nicolas Bainbridge were the only people who knew the truth. Since Angus Aherne was a child prodigy, he was sent to live with his aunt in France. Under her musical tutelage, he graduated from a private high school with honors the same year Brody had, after which he completed three years of post-secondary education, became an art dealer, and lived abroad only to return home fewer than eight times in the last decade to visit his parents while they were still alive. After Brody, his older twin, had died, Angus returned to the family home as the only surviving heir.

As for me, Angus allowed me to stay with him because Brody had left me his share of the estate and I was the only personal connection to his brother Angus had left. The story was laughable. I'm convinced that the authorities, in particular, the government, didn't believe one bogus word, but the cost to prove it would've been detrimental to their involvement in the Snuff program. Brody knew too much. It was better to let sleeping dogs lie. If Brody kept a low profile, they were willing to risk his freedom.

Voices echoed in the grand cathedral entrance, Brody's and that of a stranger, a man with a British accent. I poked my head out through the archway. The man had the build of a bulldog: wide shoulders, barrel chest, and a narrow V at the hips. He walked beside Brody in my direction. His clothes were plain, T-shirt and jeans, and he had a square profile, thick eyebrows, and bent nose. He was not attractive at all. He was one tough-looking son-of-a-bitch, and he gave off mobster vibes.

"This is Mr. Harrison," Brody said. "He's a friend of Bainbridge's."

"Nice to meet you." We shook hands, as he removed his sunglasses.

"Likewise, Zeus."

"You know my name?"

"Nickie loves to talk about you."

"Bainbridge," I said through an awkward smile.

"That's right." The guy flashed a wide, white-toothed grin.

"Let's sit in the kitchen," Brody offered, gesturing to the space behind me. "Would you like a coffee?"

"No thanks. I think it's best I get to the point."

I didn't utter a syllable as we all sat around the table. But I did keep a close eye on Brody's reaction to what the man was about to say.

"Thing is," Harrison said, inching his chair in tight by gripping it from underneath, "I work for British intelligence. And a little birdie told me that you are very good at extermination work... probably one of the best."

Brody's features remained deadpan, unresponsive. "I have no idea what you're referring to. I'm an art dealer."

"*Sure* you are." Harrison smirked, digging inside his rear hip pocket, and placed a plain white business card on the table with a snap. It had an eleven-digit number on it, printed in a small, red font. "My superiors need someone experienced to perform odd jobs. Right now, there is a certain undesirable that needs to be eliminated. He is the leader of an Asian nation, a dictator that has killed three million of his own people, and he's threatened to invade neighboring countries. Previous attempts to remove him from power have failed. No one can get close enough. And pressure from other nations is growing."

Brody glanced at the card then blinked slowly before looking the foreign agent in the eyes. "I am positive if my brother were alive, he'd find your proposal intrigu—"

"My superiors will pay all expenses plus a completion fee of one hundred thousand pounds. If you fail, they will still pay the expenses, plus twenty thousand pounds for your time and effort. Of course, they'd like to see the job done, but they understand that they must allow for human error."

"My brother never made a mistake," Brody said in a coldly contemptuous tone, his steely-gray eyes burning just slightly.

"I've heard he was remarkable."

"Scarcely human."

Harrison placed his hands on the table, rising. "I'll leave now."

I bent my arm behind my head and slouched, holding the business card to the light, while Brody escorted Harrison to the front entrance. I figured the lure of doing what ignited Brody's inmost yearnings, would be too great a temptation for him. He was still a killer at heart.

"You can dispose of that."

Scrutinizing the card, I held it between my index and middle fingers like a razor blade. "That guy sure had balls to come here. More than likely it's a trap."

"I will never do someone else's bidding again."

"And I don't want you to."

He stood at the patio slider, his expression vexed and intensely focused on the backyard. Brows furrowed, he clutched his own shirt, making a fist. "I still get the urge."

Suddenly, everything made sense. I pressed my palm to the cool glass and scanned the lush garden and tree line beyond the edge of the property. "I thought the sex was rougher than usual," I said. "And there's a paint stain on the top of your right runner. But now, I'm pretty sure it isn't paint."

"He was our mechanic. His wife had a black eye when I paid for the repair bill. I'd smelled the sour odor of stale alcohol seeping from his pores. That night I waited until he closed the shop then followed him home. He got drunk, and then beat his wife and son. Three days ago, I overheard a pair of police officers in the convenience-store. The abuse had worsened. His son is comatose in the hospital." Brody clenched his jaw, the ferocity of his grip tearing his shirt. "I lured him to the amusement park under the pretext of needing help to repair the Ferris wheel."

"The amusement park? That's a little too close for comfort, don't you think?"

"Don't worry, I made it look like an accident."

"Okay...and what did you say to lure him in?"

"My family purchased the land. I wanted to find out if the machinery is salvageable." He looked at me, his dark eyes piercing my soul in a way that made me nervous. "Do you still love me?"

It never ceased to amaze me that for all his fortitude and calculating nature, Brody could still be the most insecure person in the world. He had balls the size of Texas when it came to death and carnage, but he'd wilt emotionally if he thought I didn't care. He had changed, although he was oblivious to it.

"We've been together many years now. I'm pretty sure love isn't an issue." Admiring the view, I smacked the back of my hand against his chest before he could get another word in edgewise. "The prick deserved it. End of story. Besides, it's my birthday, and you promised to make me pancakes. I'm starving."

He eyed me and his lips parted into a rather sly grin. "Eggs?"

"Of course, sunny-side up—oh, and don't forget the sausages and orange juice." I dragged a stool out from the island and propped my head on a fist. "And that's freshly squeezed."

I smiled. I loved the sound of Brody's laughter.

Blak Rayne is an author of gay romance. She loves to write and believes it's one of the greatest forms of self-expression. What better way to see inside the human soul? Blak Rayne resides in Canada, and yes, she is a woman, wife, and mother. She's been writing and drawing since elementary school, and she loves anything that involves the arts. As for family, her daughter is her toughest critic and greatest support!

Thank you for reading *The Reaper Complete Series*! I hope you enjoyed it. Sign-up for my newsletter at www.blakraynebooks.com to receive information on my latest releases, author promotions, news-blog posts, contests, giveaways and special offers. *Radioactive*, my latest novel is coming to eXtasy Books! Did you know the best way to show an author support is by posting a review? If you liked *The Reaper Complete Series* please consider posting a review anywhere my books are sold.